W9-BDW-081

10/14

YOU
KILL ME

Other Books by Alison Gaylin

Hide Your Eyes

YOU KILL ME

Alison Gaylin

A SIGNET BOOK

SIGNET
Published by New American Library, a division of
Penguin Group (USA) Inc., 375 Hudson Street,
New York, New York 10014, USA
Penguin Group (Canada), 90 Eglinton Avenue East, Suite 700, Toronto,
Ontario M4P 2Y3, Canada (a division of Pearson Penguin Canada Inc.)
Penguin Books Ltd., 80 Strand, London WC2R 0RL, England
Penguin Ireland, 25 St. Stephen's Green, Dublin 2,
Ireland (a division of Penguin Books Ltd.)
Penguin Group (Australia), 250 Camberwell Road, Camberwell, Victoria 3124,
Australia (a division of Pearson Australia Group Pty. Ltd.)
Penguin Books India Pvt. Ltd., 11 Community Centre, Panchsheel Park,
New Delhi - 110 017, India
Penguin Group (NZ), cnr Airborne and Rosedale Roads, Albany,
Auckland 1310, New Zealand (a division of Pearson New Zealand Ltd.)
Penguin Books (South Africa) (Pty.) Ltd., 24 Sturdee Avenue,
Rosebank, Johannesburg 2196, South Africa

Penguin Books Ltd., Registered Offices:
80 Strand, London WC2R 0RL, England

First published by Signet, an imprint of New American Library,
a division of Penguin Group (USA) Inc.

ISBN 0-7394-6242-3

Copyright © Alison Sloane Gaylin, 2005
All rights reserved

 REGISTERED TRADEMARK—MARCA REGISTRADA

Printed in the United States of America

Without limiting the rights under copyright reserved above, no part of this
publication may be reproduced, stored in or introduced into a retrieval system, or transmitted, in any form, or by any means (electronic, mechanical,
photocopying, recording, or otherwise), without the prior written permission
of both the copyright owner and the above publisher of this book.

PUBLISHER'S NOTE
This is a work of fiction. Names, characters, places, and incidents either are the
product of the author's imagination or are used fictitiously, and any resem-
blance to actual persons, living or dead, business establishments, events, or lo-
cales is entirely coincidental.

The publisher does not have any control over and does not assume any re-
sponsibility for author or third-party Web sites or their content.

The scanning, uploading, and distribution of this book via the Internet or via
any other means without the permission of the publisher is illegal and pun-
ishable by law. Please purchase only authorized electronic editions, and do
not participate in or encourage electronic piracy of copyrighted materials.
Your support of the author's rights is appreciated.

To Mike.
And to Marissa, our firefighter/princess.

ACKNOWLEDGMENTS

Very special thanks go out to Detective Joe Muldoon, NYPD Retired, for answering every single question I had. Everything I got right is to his credit; everything wrong has nothing to do with him.

My gratitude also to Abigail Thomas, Jo Treggiari, The Golden Notebook, The Woodstock Wool Company . . . and all the usual suspects from the scene of the previous crime, especially and always Ellen Edwards.

Thanks as well to Debra Bard Javerbaum for brilliant Web design, Beverly Sloane and Sheldon and Marilyn Gaylin for invaluable moral support and babysitting, to my daughter Marissa Anne Gaylin for saying and doing so many wonderful, printable things. And to my husband, Mike Gaylin, whose incredible patience and ability to pick up all sorts of slack kept the title of this book from becoming prophetic.

If you stop acting like a victim, he'll stop treating you like one.
—*Sydney Stark-Leiffer,* PMS: Postmarital Survival

PROLOGUE

Now and Forever

About two months after the September 11 attacks, when the city still smelled like burning plastic and people shuffled down the sidewalks, faces blank and sad as flattened pennies, Detective John Krull and I decided to rent a car and drive out into the country.

The idea was to go to New Hope, Pennsylvania, where my former off-off-Broadway box-office colleague, Argent Devereaux, was performing in a production of *Cats*. Argent had quit her job at our theater, the Space, and moved to New Hope more than a year earlier, after winning the role of Grizabella.

Since Argent's departure, I'd killed a murderer, moved in with a cop, said good-bye to one class, hello to another at Sunny Side Preschool, where I teach the nine-to-twelve class. At the Space, where I work afternoons, we'd seen three plays open and flop. (Actually, the one-man show about Stalin's dog had been pretty clever.) Then the planes had flown into the World Trade Center, and the theater went dark indefinitely. We all lost our paychecks while the artistic director tried to figure out what type of show she could possibly put on a stage when people were still breathing in ashes.

No one wanted to let go of their kids either, so the Sunny Side was temporarily closed, giving me a lot of free time to fill. I spent most of it uptown, sitting in the lobby of the Plaza, pretending I was visiting from somewhere far away.

Several cops from Krull's precinct had died, as well as a much-loved detective from the bomb squad, which is housed in the same building. Krull started working twelve- to fifteen-hour days, spent mostly at the wreckage. Then he'd come home, attempt sleep for a few hours and head out again. We hardly spoke during that time, other than to say good-bye. But every time he left the apartment, he hugged me so tight it hurt.

By the time things started to calm down, Krull's partner Art Boyle had come out of a four-month retirement, and his other partner, Amanda

Patton, had put her baby son in day care and returned to work full-time.

Krull was perhaps the only cop I knew who had refused therapy of any sort—not even one grief-counseling session. And, try as I might to convince him otherwise, I learned that this man— who had taken a bullet in the neck for me, who had urged me to tell him everything that frightened me—was someone who did not "want to fucking *talk* about things."

Yet through it all, this smash-hit production of *Cats* in New Hope, Pennsylvania, kept playing to packed houses six nights plus one matinee performance a week, with Argent Devereaux in the starring role. No wonder that show's slogan was "Now and Forever."

Anyway, the prospect of seeing something that hadn't changed in a year was so appealing to Krull and me that we paid a ridiculous amount of money to rent a car one Saturday, booked a night at a New Hope hotel called Honeymoon Sweets and headed out on the open highway.

I don't remember much about the show itself, other than someone shouting, "Yes!" as Argent first made her entrance, wedged into a shredded unitard, glittery whiskers scrawled across her face.

As for the rest of the trip, I know Krull and I walked through a park and talked about how the bare trees reminded us of skeletons. I know we shared a split of sweet, headachy champagne from the minibar and had sex on a bed shaped like a giant heart. But I can't feel any of it, can't taste it or even see it anymore. It's a dim memory in the literal sense of the phrase—a recollection with its batteries running out.

There is one exception, though—an event from the ride home that keeps getting sharper in my mind—and it's the main reason why I'm telling the story in the first place.

Krull was driving, and we'd just turned onto a two-lane highway. There was a straight, empty stretch of road ahead of us, and we were listening to Black Sabbath on the radio when an SUV swung up behind our rental car, passed us and hit a squirrel.

It was the first time I'd ever seen roadkill happen, and what surprised me, when we passed the little body, was the tiny amount of blood and the way the head, legs and tail jolted up and down, like it was trying to signal us. "He's still alive," I said.

Krull said, "Some things keep moving a long time after they're dead."

The way he said it made me think he wasn't talking about squirrels at all. But when I looked at him, staring out the window with that jaw of his clenched, as if it might hurt to say anything more, I knew a follow-up question wasn't in the cards.

We were headed back to a burning city, after all. We'd left New Hope behind.

It's November 2002. That weekend trip was a year ago, and I've since lost the feeling of anything being "now and forever." Yes, Argent is still the Betty Buckley of New Hope. And I, Samantha Leiffer, am still teaching four-year-olds how to write their names and selling tickets to often-embarrassing theatrical productions. But it's amazing how much everything else has changed—and I'm not talking about the fact that people now walk by that great, smoldering pit in Battery Park talking on their cell phones, making dinner plans without even turning to look at it.

What I'm talking about is my own life. I'm talking about what scares me now.

On my mother's Web site, this quote is currently posted: "Everyone creates her own reality." I really hate that quote. But I must say, it's true of Sydney. She created hers twenty-five years ago, when my dad moved out. Instead of leaving me with my grandmother, checking into a motel and gorging herself on rocky road ice cream and single-malt scotch (which is what I would have done), Sydney left me with my grandmother, checked into a motel and wrote a runaway best seller: *PMS: Postmarital Survival.*

Since then, she's tweaked her created reality with three short-lived marriages, a syndicated newspaper column, two honorary degrees from respected universities, a heavily photographed series of dates with a much-younger tennis champ . . . the list is endless. Her life never stays exactly the same for more than one season.

But with the help of regular nips, tucks and injections and a long-suffering hairdresser named Vito Paradise, Sydney makes sure her exterior, by contrast, remains as *un*changed as possible. It's something the fans can latch onto. The face that never ages. The face of what they think they can get out of life.

This potent combination has made my mother more famous by the year. And now the press calls her what she's wanted to be called since her pre-*PMS* days: Sydney Stark-Leiffer, self-help guru.

Until this past January, Sydney was a self-help expert, sometimes a maven. But then she came out with her breakthrough book, *The Art of Caring*, in which she coined a new catchphrase—*sympathy vulture*. (I still don't know what it means.) Before long, she was doing weekly segments on *Oprah*, people like Jennifer Aniston started mentioning her name and poof . . . a guru was born.

I, on the other hand, did not create my own reality. Not any more than that squirrel in New Hope created the speeding SUV. To say I've gone through changes would be inaccurate. The truth is, changes have gone through me.

There was a time when I thought love was the one thing that could truly change you. Look at what it had done to my box-office coworkers. Shell Clarion, an insult factory in skintight pleather who would have gladly killed kittens for a part on *All My Children*, became a completely different person after moving in with aspiring screenwriter/yoga teacher En Henry. Sure, she was still annoying. But now she was annoyingly *domestic*. She stopped stuffing snapshots of her bikini-clad self into agents' and managers' comp-ticket envelopes. And, where she used to spew venomous comments on practically anyone within her airspace, she now channeled the negative energy into nagging En for an engagement ring and baking very bad muffins.

My best friend, Yale St. Germaine—who tended to end his most serious relationships after a day or two—had gone miraculously monogamous the moment he set eyes on his now-longtime boyfriend, Peter Steele. And Hermyn—a performance artist whose vow of silence had lasted three whole years—took back her voice and her old name of Amy Rosensweig, quit her job at the Space and moved from the East Village to Scarsdale . . . all after marrying Sal Merstein, dentist of her dreams. Last I'd heard, she'd become a stand-up comic and was working bachelorette parties throughout the tristate area.

Look at what love had done to me. I used to hate cops. But then I met Detective John Krull, and I didn't even think twice about moving into his apartment in Stuyvesant Town—a Lower East Side complex crawling with law enforcement professionals. Within weeks, Krull and I were playing poker with cops and their spouses on a regular basis. We went to their apartments for home-cooked meals, invited them over for delivered Chinese food (neither one of us could cook), took them to hideous shows at the Space and out for much-needed drinks afterward. Sometimes, we even babysat their kids.

And for the first time, love made me feel more comfortable with another person than I did alone. Krull and I went to bed every night with our arms wrapped around each other and his enormous cat, Jake, sprawled across our stomachs, breathing in and out in unison without even trying.

Even after September 11—when the regular poker games stopped and Krull got quieter, sometimes leaving our bed to stare, just stare, out the living room window—love was still there, like the body fat camels live off of when they're stuck in the desert for weeks. It made me think, *We'll get through this.*

But that was before I discovered the truth: There is an emotion more powerful than love. An emotion that looks like love, but isn't. This emotion . . . I'm not sure what to call it, but it can change your life in ways that make love seem like a twenty-dollar withdrawal from an ATM machine.

Because no matter how strong you think it is, no matter how much it turns your life around or domesticates you or gives you back your voice, no matter how much it makes you see the world from an angle you never knew existed, love—*real* love—can never kill you.

1

Too Safe

"Haven't I seen you somewhere before?" said the voice behind me. The voice was deep, with some sort of European accent—French? Belgian? Swiss? A tasteful trace of an accent, like a carefully chosen accessory. Like a black leather, three-button jacket bought brand-new at Barneys because it looked "so vintage," but costing more than I make in a year. He was probably wearing the coat too, despite it being ninety degrees outside.

"I don't think so," I said, without turning to look at either him or his inevitable coat.

I was sitting in a Starbucks at Tenth and Sixth at seven o'clock in the morning on September 2, 2002. It was the first day of school, and I was making name tags for my class, wondering how we'd all get along. I loved imagining faces to go with the names, trying to pick out the shy ones, the precocious ones, the troublemakers. After writing each name in red felt-tipped pen on a rectangle of yellow construction paper, I'd close my eyes, repeat the name in my head and attempt to visualize the student. Deep down, I suppose I enjoyed believing I was psychic. Like my superstitions, it gave me a sense of control.

Yes, I still had my superstitions. I'd had them so long they were like birthmarks, and I barely noticed them anymore. But my mother did. She wanted them removed.

A year and a half earlier, I'd stabbed a serial killer to death with a butcher knife after nearly getting murdered myself. And then, just as the residual nightmares were starting to fade, September 11 happened. I'd spent that whole day trying to track down Krull, until he wandered into our apartment at three in the morning, his dark hair gray from building ash, murmuring, "We're fucked, honey. We're all fucked."

Sydney couldn't understand how I could go through all that and still think it made a difference whether or not I walked under a ladder. She said I suffered from a disorder with a clinical term: *magical thinking.* But I didn't care. My mother lived three thousand miles away and could not physically stop me from stepping over cracks in the sidewalk. And besides, *magical thinking* didn't sound like a disorder. It sounded like a compliment.

Visualizing this new group of kids from the sound of their names was proving harder than usual, though. There was a Charlotte, an Ida, two Harrys, an Abraham. . . . When I closed my eyes, all I could see were friends of my grandmother.

"But I'm sure I know you. Look at me, please."

Man, this Eurotrash was persistent. Maybe it wasn't a come-on. Truth was, I'd heard that question many times since moving to New York from men and women, gay and straight, and only a few of them had said it because they wanted a date. Though puzzled at first, I'd soon discovered that small, dark-haired, vaguely Semitic girls like me were about as common as pretzel vendors here.

Plus, I looked a lot like my famous mother and had been in the press myself after the serial-killer incident. So there were quite a few people I'd never met who had, in fact, seen me somewhere before.

I turned and looked at the stranger with the overpriced accent. And instantly, I felt guilty for being so rude. He was young, but dressed thirty years older, in gray polyester slacks, a short-sleeved yellow oxford with a white T-shirt underneath. His black hair was short, combed, carefully parted. He had large, dark eyes and an olive complexion. Maybe he was from Puerto Rico, maybe Morocco, maybe Lebanon or Saudi Arabia. He was the type of person who got pulled aside and questioned by airport security guards, who got glared at on subways and hassled for no reason. I'm sure he'd heard the question too, but with such different inflection, such darker intent. *Haven't I seen you somewhere before?*

"I'm sorry," I said. "You probably just have me confused with someone. It happens all the time."

He took a step closer and gave me a hard, burning look that made me press up against the back of my chair. "You . . . are pretty," he said.

I forced a smile. "Pretty taken."

But the guy didn't move, just kept staring.

"Okay. So . . . bye." I looked at the door and, as if I'd willed it, Krull walked through, along with another Sixth Precinct detective, Zachary Pierce— a fellow Stuy Town resident who'd helped out on surveillance during my serial-killer case.

Krull's partners didn't like Pierce—Amanda Patton thought he had short-man's syndrome, and Art Boyle was prejudiced against Scorpios. But I didn't mind him; I saw the guy too often not to cut him some slack.

Around the same time Krull and I spent that weekend in New Hope, Pierce had sold his deceased mother's Queens duplex and moved into a small apartment in the building closest to ours. It had been vacated by a firefighter who'd died in 9/11, and Pierce had snapped it up after just one viewing. ("I think it's haunted," he'd said. "But on the plus side, it has a washer/dryer.")

Pierce and Krull became friends, meeting in the courtyard between our buildings and working out together at a nearby gym most mornings before work. Sometimes, Pierce would knock on our door with a six-pack of beer and invite himself in—usually when there was a game on TV, or when his ghost was acting up.

The thing about Zachary Pierce was that he overreacted to everything—especially himself. He was short and small boned, but he overreacted by working out so much that his neck swelled huge and his body became this collection of uncomfortable-looking bulges. And a few months ago, when he'd noticed that his hair had started to thin, he'd overreacted by shaving his head until it gleamed. I'd never seen a man more resemble a fire hydrant than Pierce, and it made me feel sorry for him. He tried so hard.

This morning, I'd told Krull that I planned to come to Starbucks before class, but still I was surprised they'd actually shown up. *He remembered.* A sense of relief rushed through me, and then I wondered what I was so relieved about.

From his shirt pocket, the stranger produced a piece of paper and put it in front of me. "I want you to have this," he said.

It had been carefully folded into a tiny, tight triangle.

"Call me when you are alone." He winked.

"Excuse me, but what part of 'I'm not available' don't you understand?"

The two detectives moved toward my table. I wanted Krull to kiss me, deeply and passionately enough to show each and every Starbucks patron just how unavailable I was, but that was not like him, not lately. I found myself envying the shoulder holster he wore under his drab blue suit coat, just because he was comfortable to have it that close.

I wanted Krull at least to say, "This guy giving you trouble?" But he didn't. Pierce did.

The stranger looked from Pierce to Krull, then raised both hands in a corny gesture of surrender and made a fast retreat for the door. *Guess he knows law enforcement when he sees it.*

"Looks like a terrorist to me," said Pierce.

Krull rolled his eyes and sat down at the table. "Only thing he was interested in terrorizing was my girlfriend."

I smiled at him. *My girlfriend.*

"What's that?" Krull pointed to the tiny paper triangle sitting next to my stack of name tags.

"His phone number." I flicked it across the

table. "Prefolded and ready for distribution. Way to make a woman feel special."

Pierce said, "Is that a new hairstyle?"

I touched my hair, still damp from my morning shower. Shoulder-length, pin-straight, parted just off center. "I don't think I've had a new hairstyle since I graduated college."

"Well," said Pierce, "you're lookin' like a stone-cold hottie."

What are you, twelve years old? "Thanks."

Pierce leaned his forearms on the table, clasping his hands together. One of the sad side effects of his workout regimen was that the bigger his arms grew, the smaller his hands looked. "I bet guys come on to you like that all the time," he said.

"Not really."

"Listen, if you weren't with John I'd be hitting on you like crazy."

I winced. It wasn't the first time Pierce had said this to me. And I had no doubt it was true—if only because I was one of the few adult women in New York City who was shorter than him.

"You want to step outside, buddy?" said Krull mildly.

"Hey, I said if she wasn't with you."

"Ah." Krull twirled the paper triangle between his fingers and gazed at the list of coffee flavors over the counter in a way that made me think he'd rather be anywhere but here.

We'd had a fight the previous night. Basically the same fight we'd been having every couple of weeks—if you could call something that one-sided a fight. This time, we'd been loading the dishwasher after dinner when I said, "You were so quiet tonight. Is anything wrong?"

"No. I'm fine."

"I don't believe that."

Then came the long pause, the pause he never felt the need to fill.

"John, please tell me what's on your mind. I can't help you if you won't let me in."

"I don't need your help."

"We . . . we . . . shouldn't have moved in together. Because I've never felt so alone as I feel living under the same roof with . . . I'm sorry. I didn't mean that."

He said something I couldn't hear, and I thought, *Is he talking to me, or to himself?*

"What did you just say?"

Krull removed the Tupperware bowl I'd just put in the dishwasher. "Don't load plastic on the bottom shelf," he said. "It melts." Then he left the apartment—walked out into a raging summer thunderstorm, and didn't come back for four hours.

When he returned, I was in bed, but awake. I shut my eyes anyway.

Krull stripped down to his boxers and climbed in beside me. "Sorry," he whispered. "I just needed time alone." His hair was damp, and his skin smelled like city rain and sweat. When he kissed me, I tasted cigarettes.

In all the time I'd known him, I'd never actually seen Krull smoke—only tasted it on him. I didn't ever mention it, though. I couldn't let him know I was onto the smoking, because it was one of the few ways I could gauge how upset he really was.

Funny how living with a detective can turn you into one.

Pierce said, "So you must be happy about your mother moving to New York."

It took me several seconds to digest the sentence. "What?!"

"I thought I heard it on the radio. I could be wrong, but I don't think so. Dr. Sydney Stark-Leiffer, right? *The Art of Caring?*"

"Number one, she's not a doctor. Two, I'm sure my mother would tell me if she were—"

"She's not a doctor?"

"You must've heard wrong. You—"

"Look at this," said Krull.

I stared at Pierce, amazed to absolute silence that, fight or no fight, someone I'd shared a bed with for a year and a half could hear this news— this life-altering, potentially catastrophic news involving my *mother*—and interrupt it with a directive as irritatingly dismissive as "Look at this." What was he looking at anyway, a dessert? An unusual hairstyle?

Pierce didn't seem to get it, though. "What?" he said.

I turned to Krull. He had opened the paper triangle. *So that's what's so important. Some guy's phone number.*

He handed it over.

There was indeed a phone number on the small slip of paper, but no name to go with it. Just a sentence, printed in neat, capital letters with a red felt-tipped pen similar to my own: YOU ARE IN DANGER.

Pierce said, "You guys get out of here. I'm calling the bomb squad."

There was no bomb in Starbucks. I could've told them that. I mean, what kind of terrorist leaves his phone number on a bomb-threat note? And while we're at it, if the guy had indeed wanted to warn me, wouldn't he have written something a little more specific than *You are in danger?* Something like . . . I don't know . . . *Get the fuck out of here; there's a bomb?*

I'd tried explaining that to Krull and Pierce as we stood outside the glass door with all the terrified customers and coffee servers, watching one of the bomb squad guys dissemble an espresso machine. But neither of them would listen. "You can never be too safe," Krull said.

"Yes, you can," I said. "We're too fucking safe right now."

Krull didn't say much more after that—not even after the café was officially declared explosive-free. By then, forty-five minutes had passed, and we all had to go to work.

"I probably jumped to conclusions," Pierce said. "It's just . . . The guy struck me as hinky, and after everything you've been through, Sam. . . ."

Krull's eyes narrowed. "Can I have the note?"

"What are you going to do now?" I said. "Handwriting analysis?"

"Reverse directory."

I looked at Krull. "You gonna pay Monsieur Perp a little *visite? Teach le skel* how to say *danger* in American?"

He grinned. No matter how strained things were between us, I could always get a smile out of him with bad cop dialogue.

He gave me a quick kiss on the lips. "Affirmative," he said before leaving, with Pierce, for the Sixth Precinct. For a few seconds, I stood there on the sidewalk, watching as they walked away. Pierce was the only one to look back.

"Well, who isn't in danger?" said Yale St. Germaine. "He may as well have given you a note that says, 'You breathe.'"

I shrugged my shoulders. "Got my attention,

though. I bet plenty of women would have called him, if only out of morbid curiosity."

Yale and I were in my classroom, taping name tags to the kids' cubbyholes and straightening books, dusting off chairs and tabletops, inventorying the art supplies closet, all in preparation for the first day of school.

When I'd started teaching here four years earlier, I'd been so nervous on day one that I'd had to change shirts three times. In a state of panic, I'd called Yale, screaming, *"My deodorant isn't working!"* Clearly sensing deeper underlying feelings, he had offered to show up an hour before the kids arrived to keep me company and help get everything organized. The moment he walked through the door, I'd stopped sweating, and without either of us suggesting the idea out loud, it became an annual tradition for him to join me on the first day and stay until the class got settled.

This time around, I'd shown up ten minutes late to find Yale waiting outside the classroom door—a first. When he asked where I'd been, I'd replied simply, "Bomb scare."

"Were the bomb squad cops hot, at least?" Yale said now. "I've always found *detonate* to be an incredibly sexy word."

"I was too pissed off to look at them. I swear, Pierce needs to be on a leash." *And John Krull shouldn't be allowed to hold it.*

Immediately, I wanted to take back the thought. *He's been through so much. He's bound to overreact. He wants to be safe, wants me to be safe.*

But Jesus. The bomb squad? In Starbucks? Since when did he start buying into Pierce's craziness?

I then heard Sydney's voice in my head, clear as if she were standing next to me: *"Hypervigilance is classic overcompensation."*

"Meaning?"

"He's having an affair and he feels guilty. Don't be so naive, Samantha. Where does a man go for four hours in the middle of the night in the pouring rain?"

"That's it!" Yale slammed both hands on the bookshelf, and my skin jumped.

"What's it?"

"Marketing campaign!"

"Huh?"

"You know . . . the little man hands out these notes to pretty girls, maybe boys too. They say, 'You are in danger.' You call the number and it turns out Danger is the name of a club."

I looked at him. "Then shouldn't the note say, 'You *will be* in danger'?"

"English isn't his first language, Sam." Yale went back to alphabetizing storybooks.

"I bet you're right," I said—not because I thought he was, but because a marketing campaign for a nightclub fronted by the likes of that guy, in those clothes, made about as much sense as anything else did today.

I taped up my last name tag: Ezra. *"That was my great-uncle's name, and by the way, John Krull is not cheating on me, and you'd better not be moving to New York."*

"Yale," I said, "have you heard any news lately? About my mother?"

"Good lord, is she getting married again?"

"Pierce said he thought it was on the radio that she's moving. Here."

He rolled his eyes. "If that were true, wouldn't she have told you herself, rather than have you hear it from Captain Orange Alert?"

"I . . . hope." I knocked on the wooden desk for good luck, and, at the exact same time, someone knocked on the door.

"That had better not be a terrorist," Yale said.

"I beg your pardon, may I?" It was the voice of Terry Mann, Sunny Side's principal.

"He's so polite it's borderline psychotic," whispered Yale, who delighted in using Terry's formal appellation. "Hel-lo, Mr. Mann!"

Like a cat, Terry nudged open the door and stepped in. "Hello, Yale. Samantha, I wanted to remind you that both Ezra and Harry W. have peanut allergies, so please snack accordingly."

Terry smiled. In the entire time I'd known the principal, I'd probably seen him smile five times, counting this one. It always looked painful, like a contortion he'd been practicing every day for months, but still hadn't quite gotten the hang of.

"I hope everybody likes cinnamon graham crackers and apple juice," I said. That's what I'd put in the small refrigerator that occupied a corner of the storage closet. It's what I always put in there on the first day of class and what we had for snack time for about 90 percent of the school year, except on those rare occasions when I got creative and bought string cheese and grapes.

Terry said, "By the way, I saw your mother on television."

"Why?!" said Yale and I, a little too loudly.

He stepped back, bracing himself against the bookshelf as if we were a strong, unpleasant wind. "I didn't hear her. I just saw her . . . through the window of an electronics store. I believe she was being interviewed."

Yale put a hand on my shoulder. "Your mother's always being interviewed on TV. She's not moving to New York."

I knocked wood again.

"I don't have a television of my own," said Terry. "But I enjoy her books very much—especially *Your Spiritual Lifeboat.* Very clever indeed."

I sensed movement behind Terry—a few of Veronica Bliss's students arriving in the classroom next to mine. *Well, they're early,* I thought, until I glanced at my watch and saw it was nearly nine o'clock.

"It's showtime, folks," said Yale. I held my breath, closed my eyes and counted to seven in my head seven times for good luck. Fortunately no one noticed me.

When I opened my eyes, Terry had already begun to greet my new kids and their parents as they filed in.

There was blond, freckle-faced Ida Burroughs, who dragged her mother by the arm like an oversize doll. There was dark-eyed, shy Charlotte Weiss and her peanut-averse twin, Harry, his face damp from tears, both clinging to the legs of their British au pair (a sturdy, serious-looking teenager who introduced herself as Soph). Next came Ezra Sargent, redheaded and classically cute, shouting out an obviously rehearsed, "Hello, I'm Ezra, I'm four and a half years old and I love learning!"

Now there's a Professional Children's School candidate if I ever saw one.

Then Yale said, "Holy shhhhh . . ." like a punctured tire, and what little color was there to begin with rushed out of Terry's face.

Yale didn't finish the word—Terry and I both sighed in gratitude for that; I was relatively sure Soph did as well. But when I saw the man sauntering in and standing behind Ezra—yet grinning at me as if I were the only other person in the room—I nearly completed the word myself and added two exclamation points.

It took me a few seconds to get my mouth to open, a few more before I found enough breath to say his name. "Nate?"

Yale said, "You're in danger, all right."

2

All About Me

Nate Gundersen was my first love, the first guy I ever lived with and, according to Yale, empirical proof that I was just as shallow as anyone else.

Granted, Nate was stunning—golden haired and amber eyed and perfect in a way that bordered on the absurd. But it wasn't his looks that had drawn me in. It was, to be precise, his *look*. It was the look in his eyes, backstage during dress rehearsal of our college production of *King Lear*, when he'd asked if I could help him get his clothes off between scenes.

Yes, he had a quick costume change. And yes, I was the stage manager. But that look—the look he gave me in the darkened wing of Stanford University's Pigott Theater, with one worklight pouring over the sculpted length of him—had nothing to do with stages or managing. A subtle lift of his eyebrow, and I was at the top of a roller coaster, staring ahead at the plunging track. *Hold on tight and get ready to scream.*

It was some look.

And there it was again, in front of my boss and my best friend and a bunch of four-year-olds I'd never met before, years after Nate had hurt me so much I'd vowed to hate him forever.

"Well, if it isn't Mr. Versatility," said Yale, who was not in any way referring to Nate's talent as an actor on the daytime soap opera *Live and Let Live.*

"Mr. *Gundersen!*" said Ezra. "He's my uncle and he's a star!"

"Real uncle or Mommy's special friend?" said Yale. "Or perhaps you're *Daddy's* spec—"

Luckily I was standing close enough to kick him. "Sorry."

"Yale, right?" *There goes that damn eyebrow.*

I glanced at Yale. He was actually blushing.

"Very nice to meet you both." Terry glared at me. "This is Samantha, Ezra's teacher, who I'm sure intended to introduce herself, didn't you?"

"Samantha and I know each other," said Nate. "In fact, that's why I convinced Jenna to let me drop off Ez."

"Jenna Sargent—the actress," said Yale.

"That's right," said Nate. "She's not my real sister, but she plays her on TV."

"You're on television?" said Terry.

"I'll say!" said Soph. "I watch you every day, and I can't believe you're babysitting Blythe's son after she tried to murder you!"

"Blythe is just a character, you ignoramus," said Ezra.

"Soph is not a ickeranus!" yelled Harry. Then both twins flew at Ezra like avenging bats.

The first fight of the school year and no one even had their name tags yet. This must have been some kind of Sunny Side record—one I knew Veronica Bliss would take great pleasure in gloating over as soon as she found out. But as Terry, Yale, Soph and I struggled to pry the kids apart, with Ida Burroughs and her mother saying, "Oh, my God" at the exact same time and Nate apologizing to someone (I wasn't sure who), I realized I was glad for the fight. I was glad to have something—apart from my ex—on which to focus my attention.

Because, the truth was, I hadn't said a word since his name. And when I did—if I did—who knew what that word would be?

As it turned out, it wasn't a word, but a noise—the kind someone might make if they'd been raised by wolves and had eaten bad carrion.

"Hello, Green Eyes," said Nate.

"Uggghhhmmph." At least I hadn't said it was good to see him.

We were standing just outside my classroom door. Inside, Terry was lecturing Ezra and the twins as more kids started to show up. I could hear Yale introducing himself as "the temporary teacher's aide." I knew I had to get back inside soon.

Over Nate's shoulder, I saw Veronica stick her head out of her classroom door, then pull it back fast, like a huge toe testing cold water.

Why was Nate Gundersen smiling? Did he think that what he'd done to me didn't matter anymore? Did he honestly believe there was statute of limitations on bisexual cheating?

"It's so weird," he said. "I had this dream about you the other night. More of a memory, actually, from when we were driving cross-country on our way to New York. We were at that sleazy little motel just outside of Phoenix, remember? With the caved-in bed? You called it—"

"The Grand Canyon."

"Right. And we slept in it. Took us a long time to work everything out so we were comfortable in that pit without crushing each other. But never once did we think about switching rooms. That's how young we were."

Now it was Yale's turn to stick his head out the door. "You all right, Sam?"

"I'm fine." *You had sex with Susan, the commercial agent, every weekday between ten and noon. Gregory, the theatrical agent, was Monday, Wednesday and Friday at six. God knows who you penciled in for afternoons, for weekends.*

Nate said, "Ever feel older than you are? Sometimes I think this city has aged me in dog years."

That evening Method acting class that kept running late. The hang-ups on the answering machine. Those flowers, from Gregory, with the note: "For a job well-done." "What job?" I asked you, hating the way my voice betrayed me by cracking.

"You know, you're the only woman I've ever met who could beat me in a staring contest."

"Okay. I give up. What the fuck are you doing here?"

"Samantha." He said my name like it was his favorite dish.

I gritted my teeth. "You've got ten seconds."

"Babe," he said, "you're not making this very eas—"

"One, two, three . . ."

"I came to ask forgiveness."

I should've known from the way he'd phrased it. Nate never said things like "ask forgiveness." Nobody did. It sounded to me like a memorized line from a tired old script—which, in all reality, it was. Nate—the reason why I'd moved from California to New York, the man who had once said, "I can't wait until we're old and retired so we can spend all day in bed together"—was twelve-stepping for sex addiction.

And I was step seven.

I wasn't quite sure what annoyed me more: the fact that Nate was such a slut that he had to join an organized program just to keep his dick in his pants, or that he'd come to my *preschool classroom* to tell me about it.

Two hours after I'd asked him to get out of my workplace and never come back, my jaw was starting to ache from all the stored tension.

Still, I was trying to focus on my class, which was now hard at work on "All About Me" collages. Veronica Bliss had told me about the collages the previous fall. She'd gotten the idea from a teaching magazine, and had found them a creative way to get to know her kids, plus ease them back into school after 9/11. It was the first (and last) time she'd given a helpful suggestion that didn't have the dual purpose of insulting me, which gave it an added resonance.

Immediately, I started saving magazines for this year: more or less every non-X-rated publication from my neighborhood newsstand that didn't feature pictures of burning towers. By now, I'd accumulated close to two hundred, which I'd stacked in piles on the floor of the bedroom closet, between my four pairs of shoes and the small, squat safe where Krull stored his service revolver.

With his help, I'd brought them here days earlier, and he was clearly relieved to be rid of them. One August morning, the two tallest stacks had fallen on Krull's head while he was working the combination on the safe, causing something close to a mild concussion. After I dug him out of the wreckage, he'd said, "Sam, when you take an idea and run with it, you have a tendency to run a little too far."

"I'm sorry, honey, but the kids need a choice."

And a choice they now had. Charlotte Weiss—who wanted to be a firefighter/princess when she grew up—was paging frantically through several issues of *Disney Adventures* magazine, using one of the dull pairs of scissors to free every available rendering of *Beauty and the Beast*'s Belle. Abraham Cooper, on the other hand, favored *Car and Driver* and *TIME*'s space-travel issue, while Ida Burroughs had covered her entire piece of construction paper with cat-food ads.

I'd made my own "All About Me" collage earlier and stuck it to the wall as an example. Green construction paper (my favorite color) with glued-on pictures of a California beach scene, the New York City skyline, a scoop of chocolate ice cream, a still from my favorite movie, *The Wizard of Oz*, and a newspaper photo of the Central Park Zoo polar bear, sleeping peacefully in a snowstorm. Nothing gave me more hope than that picture. If that bear—hundreds of thousands of miles away from his natural habitat on a patch of fake land too small for him even to run across—could find contentment in a lousy blizzard, then there were endless possibilities for the rest of us. To my class, though, I'd simply said, "I love polar bears."

I glanced at Ezra, who had appropriated a February *Entertainment Weekly* and was cutting out a full-page photo of an Oscar.

Not surprisingly (if you know four-year-olds), Ezra had quickly made peace with the Weiss twins. In fact, he was now sitting next to Harry W., the boys having bonded over their mutual admiration of Thomas the Tank Engine.

Why couldn't grown-ups forgive and forget like kids? *Because kids never pick up a phone in the middle of the night to hear some strange woman's voice, sobbing, "He told me he was single."*

Should I tell Krull about seeing Nate today? I closed my eyes, tried to visualize his response. . . .

"I've always hated Nate Gundersen."

"I'm surprised you remember his name."

"How could I forget the name of that moron? He had the most wonderful woman in the world and blew it. How could he cheat on you? I would never cheat on you—never, ever, ever, ever."

Krull has changed out of his work clothes, locked his

gun in the safe. He's wearing a black T-shirt and those tight jeans with the hole in the knee, and he's lying on the bed, looking up at me. "You know where I was last night?"

"Where?"

He rips off the shirt.

"Walking around Manhattan, thinking about how I don't deserve you. Unfortunately, it was late and no jewelry stores were open, but . . ." Off come the jeans and boxers as one.

"Let me make it up to you now. Let me give you what you deserve." He pulls me onto the bed and pins me down while his lips seek—

"Ms. Leiffer, I need more kitties!" said Ida.

"And I need more Academy Awards!"

"Oh . . . sure," I thumbed through one of the stacks, searching for unnoticed issues of *Cat Fancy* and *Premiere,* all the while thanking God that kids couldn't read minds.

"Are you hot?"

I looked up, and there was Veronica, hovering just behind my head like a swarm of gnats.

"Excuse me?" I said.

"Terry needs to do something about the air-conditioning, don't you think?"

"Oh. Maybe. Are you guys hot?"

A few of my kids shook their heads, but Veronica didn't bother looking. "Speaking of hot. I happened to notice Nate Gundersen."

Did it take her two whole hours to come up with that one? "Yep."

"He was here."

"Yep."

She glanced at the kids, then leaned in close. "But he dumped you," she stage-whispered.

"Actually, that wasn't the way it happened," I whispered back.

"What does *dumped* mean?" said Charlotte.

Her brother replied, "It means poo-poo."

A few predictable giggles.

"No, it doesn't," said Ezra.

"Yes, it does."

"No, it doesn't!"

I grabbed a November *People* and threw it in front of Ezra. "Look! Emmys!" I pulled Veronica toward the door. "Thanks for the idea," I said, while trying to ease her out.

"Idea?"

"The 'All About Me' collages. The kids love making them."

Veronica swatted the words away, then suddenly leaned in so close that all I could see were reflections of my face in her glasses. For half a second, I was terrified she might kiss me. But instead she said, "Be careful."

Oh, please. The day Nate "dumped" me was three months after I'd started teaching at Sunny Side. He'd been due to meet me there for lunch, after my class let out. But he never showed up. Half an hour after my last kid had gone home, I'd called our apartment from the pay phone outside Terry's office and started leaving a message for Nate on our answering machine.

"Hi. It's me, and I'm wondering where—"

Click.

"Sorry, but Nate can't come to the phone right now." The voice was female, filled with laughter and breath.

I let the receiver drop from my hand and stared at it, dangling from the thick silver cable. I could hear Nate's voice struggling out, small and desperate as the voice of a shrunken man in a science-fiction movie. "Samantha? Samantha!"

I wanted to choke the life out of the cord, to slam the receiver against the wall. "Fuck you, Nate."

"Did you just say the F-word?" Veronica was standing behind me, but at the time I knew her only as the Nine-to-Five Teacher. And all I knew *about* her was that she made more money than me, and had two aides. She was wearing a white blouse with a playing-card pattern. I couldn't stop staring at the queen of hearts—so smooth featured, so smug.

"No matter how upset we are, we must watch the potty talk," she said. "Little ears are always near."

If the queen of hearts had a voice, I thought, *she would sound exactly like the Nine-to-Five Teacher.*

"Believe it or not, I'm actually over Nate Gundersen, Veronica."

"Miss Leiffer! Ida took my glue!"

"I mean it. I don't give a flying fudgecake about him anymore, so . . . see ya." But Veronica stayed still, and I began debating whether or not it was against some kind of school code to physically push a fellow teacher out of my classroom.

Bless her, she budged. But just as I was about to close the door, Veronica gave me a look—her eyes glinting with an emotion I'd never seen in her. "I didn't mean be careful of Nate Gundersen," she said. "I meant . . . *be careful.*"

Then she reached into her pocket and removed something small enough to disappear in her closed fist, which she held out to me tentatively.

It was one of those rare times when I didn't just believe I was psychic; I *knew* it. Because, in those few seconds before she opened her hand, I knew what would be in it. I found my voice again just as her fingers stretched out like thick petals, and if nothing else, you had to admire how synchronized it all was. "Did a foreigner give you that?" I said, at the exact moment it revealed itself at the center of her palm . . . a white piece of paper, folded into a tiny, tight triangle.

3

Reverie

He'd given the note to Veronica that morning, she explained. She'd been busy unlocking the school's front door when someone had tapped her on the shoulder, sending a shock through her nervous system, the remnants of which would most likely stay lodged in her lower spine for weeks.

"I just know I'll have to go to the chiropractor again, and insurance won't even cover it!" Veronica said, eyeing me in a challenging way, as if she planned to sue.

"When did you say he came?" That's what interested me most. The time frame.

The stranger had tapped her on the shoulder a full hour before I arrived at Sunny Side. Which meant he'd probably gone there directly from Starbucks. Which meant he hadn't followed me; he already knew where I worked.

"He said, 'Please give this to Miss Samantha Leiffer,'" said Veronica. "And . . . well, you know how I am. To each his own. Whomever you want to spend off hours with is your business, as long as it doesn't affect the children, but—"

"Veronica, I don't know that man. I've only seen him once before, and that was this morning. In Starbucks."

"Miss Leiffer!" Ida shouted. "Abraham said my collage is the S-word!"

"But it *is* stupid!"

"Abraham, we don't use that word. Apologize to Ida, please." I looked at Veronica.

"Well, he seemed to know *you*," she said. "And that was bothersome, because he's obviously . . . exotic. And when he looked at me, he had a lascivious gleam in his eye." She glanced back at the kids, then lowered her voice. "I think he's dangerous."

If ever there was an unreliable narrator, it was Veronica—a thirty-seven-year-old virgin who still lived with her parents and wouldn't know *lascivious* if it took her out to dinner and jumped her from behind.

"He didn't strike me as dangerous," I said. "He ran away from John."

She gave me a long, appraising look, followed by a heavy sigh. "Open your eyes, Samantha," she said, and headed for her classroom.

Slowly, I walked back to my desk, placing the triangle on top without opening it.

As I made my way to the long table where the kids were working on their collages, I noticed Ezra had been watching me. "Is that your fortune?" he asked, pointing to the note.

You are in danger.

Behind my back, I crossed the fingers on both hands, then crossed the wrists too, to make it an odd number—always luckier unless you're talking thirteen. "I hope not," I said.

"Open your eyes, Samantha." Veronica's words looped through my mind for the rest of the afternoon. When the most sheltered woman in all of New York City patronizes you, it tends to stick.

The note was in the back pocket of my jeans, but still I hadn't opened it yet—hadn't wanted to in class, though I wouldn't have had the chance anyway.

A glue fight between Ida and Abraham had turned very ugly very fast and, though I'd managed to separate them, I'd emerged with my favorite pale green T-shirt a gooey mess, and a clump of my hair epoxied to a collarbone.

After enduring a series of suspicious looks

from parents—not to mention Soph, who called me a "bloody horror show, if you don't mind my saying"—I'd pulled my crusty hair back with a rubber band until the last parent (Ezra's nanny, Soccoro) left the building.

Then I ran to the new Gap across the street and bought the only shirt I could afford—a plain white tank top—which I wore out of the dressing room, ripping off the tags as I waited in line to buy it.

"You know who you look like?" said the girl manning the cash register. "Dr. Sydney Stark-Leiffer."

I cringed. "She's not a doctor."

Only then did I realize I'd left both my old shirt and my purse back in the dressing room.

After I was done waiting in the cash register line all over again, I headed for a pay phone just outside the store, and used my memorized phone card number to call my mother's cell. When I got her voice mail, I said, "I know this sounds weird, but are you moving to New York? Someone told me he heard—" I would have said more. At the very least, I would have finished the sentence.

But an unmistakable feeling halted my train of thought: eyes, boring into my back. Someone was watching me.

I've always hated the way some people stare at you when you're on a public phone—as if it's their personal property and you're abusing a privilege. "Talk to you later, Mom," I said. "There's someone behind me who is *obviously* waiting."

I hung up. "It's all yours."

When I turned around, though, I saw there was no one waiting behind me.

Looking up and down the busy sidewalk, I didn't see one person who even returned my gaze. So, while I still felt weirdly observed, I chalked it up to nerves. I hadn't slept much the previous night, and I tended to go a little paranoid when I got less than six hours.

As I walked to the Space, that sensation eventually dissipated, only to be replaced by one nearly as unsettling: the plastic sales tag from my new tank top, needling into my shoulder blade. In hell, everyone's clothes probably have little, plastic tags that can't be removed.

I need scissors, I thought. Which made me think of paper, which made me think of the triangle-shaped note Veronica had given me. I stopped walking and took it out of my back pocket.

I was on Sixth Avenue near Twelfth Street. To my left, I saw Ruby Redd's Brewing Company, where Yale's boyfriend, Peter, worked as a waiter, and I knew the Sixth Precinct was on Twelfth, just half a block away. "Our husbands' offices are practically next door to each other," Yale had once remarked, even though no one else would've called them offices. And no one else would've called them husbands.

The note clung to my palm. Without thinking any more about it, I turned left on Twelfth.

The heat was making people walk very slowly; it was like moving in a dream. I pushed myself through the thick, moist air, weaving around groups of pedestrians as if they lived in some different, less urgent dimension. When I finally reached the Sixth Precinct house, I was sweating so much I left handprints on the glass door.

Inside, it was less busy than usual, and there was no relief from the heat; the air-conditioning seemed to be down. A group of vaguely familiar-looking cops nodded at me as they walked slowly past, sweating into their blue uniforms and saying something about Yankees tickets.

I spotted the imposingly tall desk sergeant, Gayle Cruz, and made a beeline for her. Gayle wore her hair in long cornrows, and today she'd woven gold and silver beads into them, making her look even more coolly regal than usual. She couldn't have been more than twenty-five, yet Gayle was the type of person it seemed natural to call "your honor." She probably scared the shit out of her blind dates.

"Think you can cheer him up?" she said.

"What do you mean?"

"Never mind." She picked up her phone, told

Krull I was here to see him, and went back to the report she was filling out.

I stared at the officer long enough to make anyone feel uncomfortable. Anyone except her.

"He'll be right down."

Cheer him up. From what? His job? Me? "Got scissors?"

After I snipped the offending tag, I sat down in one of the plastic chairs near Gayle's desk and stared at the note in my hand.

Without a doubt, the best place to read a message that says, *You are in danger* is a police precinct, so I began to undo the guy's meticulous folding job. Tight as origami, it took more time and effort than anticipated. And, the more seconds elapsed in its unfolding, the more nervous I became about what was written inside. I wondered if that hadn't been the stranger's intention all along.

Once I got it open, I smoothed the paper out on my lap, closed my eyes, held my breath and thought, *One, two, three, four, five, six, seven.* The luckiest odd number there is.

Only then did I read it.

I was sure the phone number at the bottom of the second note was the same one as on the first. But the message was different, and though they were of the same red ink, the capital letters were larger, more uneven. Written in a hurry. Plus, he'd added five exclamation points—which troubled me more than the words themselves: DON'T SHOW THIS TO HIM!!!!!

Okay . . .

Who did he mean by *him?* I imagined the man watching through Starbucks' window as I quizzed Pierce about my mother and Krull slowly opened the first note.

So maybe he meant Krull. Maybe he didn't want me telling my detective boyfriend about his weird campaign to mind-fuck me into calling him. That made sense. But why such desperation? Why five exclamation points?

Across from Gayle's desk, the stairwell door pushed open. "Hey."

I studied Krull as if I were seeing him for the first time. The long, muscular legs, the broad shoulders encased in that tired old polyester suit, the loosened tie with the golf clubs on it—his father's tie circa 1978—wide and slack against the beige shirt, collar unbuttoned to accommodate the sinewy neck.

During Krull's downtime, he dressed better—a little on the dull side, but always in natural fibers. His work suits, however, were bought once every couple of years from a discount outlet on Ninety-sixth Street because, as he put it, "You have to boil clothes to get death-smell out, and I'm not gonna cook a five-hundred-dollar suit."

Whatever he wore, though, John Krull looked

best with his clothes off. *I'll show him the note, he'll put my mind at ease and tonight we can find other ways to relieve tension.*

"I've got something to show you . . ." I said, but when I looked at his face, my breath caught in the back of my throat and the words dissolved.

The hinge of Krull's jaw pressed against the skin, and his lips seemed thinner, paler than usual. But what hit me hardest were his eyes. They seemed to bore through me and stare directly at the wall, as if I were nothing more than noise. As if I didn't exist.

I'd never seen him look at anyone like that before, and, for that moment, John Krull became a stranger—someone I didn't want to know.

"What do you want to show me?" he said.

I shoved the note back into my jeans pocket. "My new shirt. You like it?"

"It's nice. That's why you're here?"

"Well, also . . . ummm . . . guess who came to Sunny Side today?"

"Who?"

"Nate Gundersen."

His eyes went from my face to his hands and back again. But that expression never changed. "Who's Nate Gundersen?" he said.

I decided to take a taxi to the Space. Better to spend a few bucks on cab fare than show up twenty minutes late when we finally had a hit on-stage. Roland, the ticketing manager, would have yelled at me, and getting yelled at was exactly the last thing I needed today.

Our hit, a musical called *Shakespearean Idol*, had been dubbed "the most inexplicable success in theatrical history" by the *New York Times* and "the stink bomb that soared" by the *Post*. It was a modern-day version of *Romeo and Juliet*, in which the doomed, star-crossed lovers were finalists on a televised talent show. Yet, although the reality of this play was even worse than its description, *Shakespearean Idol* had been playing to packed houses since opening night.

As far as I could see, the primary draw was the finale. After the lovers finally killed themselves, the talent show host picked one audience member at random to be the next idol of Verona. The red-faced idol was then pulled onstage and forced to sing the closing number, " 'Til Death."

Yale said the scene turned our theater into "some kind of fascist karaoke bar," and I had to agree. But it always earned a standing ovation, landed us on Page Six when the idol was a B-list celebrity—and, most important to Roland, sold piles and piles of tickets. For the first time since I started working at the Space, the box office staff actually had to be at work on time every day.

Fortunately, I hailed a cab with no problem,

and traffic was moving. Also, the cab was air-conditioned, and the radio was set to an all-news station. Maybe my luck was turning.

I sat back, felt the cool vinyl against my bare shoulders and started, finally, to calm down. *So Krull is in a crabby mood. Big deal.*

I closed my eyes. On the radio, the traffic report ended, followed by a commercial for a prescription antidepressant, which reminded me, again, of my mother, who often suggested I take them. *She's not going to move here without telling you. You're her only child. No one's that self-absorbed.*

A jazzy, instrumental version of "Stormy Weather" wafted out of the speakers behind me, as a sultry female voice-over asked, "Ever feel alone in a crowd?"

"Who the hell doesn't?" the cabdriver muttered.

"Do you find you can't speak to anyone, even loved ones? Are you awkward in social gatherings? Have your moods affected your work? Your sex life?"

That wasn't a crabby mood. It was something else.

"If so, you may suffer from social anxiety disorder."

At the precinct, I'd asked Krull out to lunch—not because I wanted to. I wasn't even hungry, and it would have made me late for work. "Want to have lunch with me?" I'd said, to plug up the silence.

"No, thanks. Already ate."

"John, what's wr—"

"I'm actually kind of busy right now. Sorry."

His mouth smiled, but not his eyes.

"John, wait."

"Yeah?"

I shot a quick look at Gayle, then moved closer. "Last night . . . what I said . . . about us living together . . . I didn't mean that."

"We all do things we don't mean to do." His eyes were dry, black stones.

"Rest assured, there is hope for sufferers of even the most severe symptoms."

"Things we don't mean to do." What was that supposed to mean?

"This little pill could change your life," the voice-over said, "It changed mine."

Does he want to change his life? Has he changed it already?

The last notes of "Stormy Weather" played out alone, and I thought, *Where does a man go for four hours in the middle of the night in the pouring rain?*

I wished I had enough money to quit my job at the Space and stay in this cab forever. Or at least, rent it to sleep in for a few hours.

"Recapping today's top stories, a woman's stabbed, mutilated body was found early this morning in Washington Square Park. . . ."

I opened my eyes.

"Jesus," said the cabdriver.

"She has been identified as Marla Soble, age twenty-nine, an accountant described by her neighbors at 122 West Twenty-sixth Street as kind, generous and fun-loving. She was also known for her volunteer work at the city's animal shelters. . . ."

"That's it!" I said.

The driver glanced at me, but turned quickly back around without saying a word. Who could blame him? Who knew what my face looked like with that chill running through me—that strange mix of shock and sudden fear and the misplaced satisfaction of having figured out something awful? My eyes probably looked exactly like Krull's. Of course he needed cheering up. He'd known about this murder. He'd probably caught this case.

One twenty-two West Twenty-sixth Street. My old address.

But still, why hadn't he told me?

Yale and I were stationed at the ticket window, and since the line of *Shakespearean Idol* fans stretched past the end of the block, it was a slow process telling him everything that had happened today.

"Oh, my God, another note?" Yale said. Then, in a completely different voice, "You don't *really* want me to tell you whether Corky and Juliana kill themselves, do you? That would spoil the surprise ending!"

I found the conversation irritating and kind of pointless, like pouring out your soul to someone with split-personality disorder. But it was the way Yale and I talked when we were working the window these days.

"You two look like you could use a homemade protein bar," said Shell Clarion's voice behind us.

"No, thank you," we both said in unison.

"Oh, come on, you assholes. They're gluten-free."

I turned around. Shell was holding a plastic baking tray lined with bars the color of cigarette ash.

"Did she mention my nuts are the main ingredient?" shouted En from the other room.

"He's just pissed off because I've been withholding sex for three weeks."

I said, "Okay, now we've officially been given too much information."

"No ring, no *schwing*, En! Why buy the cow when you can get the milk for free?"

"Would you deny me food as well?" En yelled. "Would you deny me water and air?!"

"I bet you'd get that ring if you denied him protein bars," said Yale.

Shell said, "Very funny. Ha, ha, ha. I'm laughing so hard I can hardly breathe."

Riiiing.

"Shell Clarion!" shouted Roland, the ticketing manager. "If you don't get your baked goods back in the subscription room and answer that phone, you are fired, effective immediately!"

"May I have two tickets for December eighteenth?" a man at my window was saying. "They don't need to be together."

I picked up the heavy binder that Roland kept next to the window, and began paging through December seating charts.

"So, did you show the note to John?" Yale asked.

"Well, yes and no . . . It looks like we're sold out that night."

"What do you mean, yes and no?" said Yale.

"What do you mean you're sold out?" said my customer. "That's four months in advance."

"It's a popular show at a small theater, sir." I looked at Yale. "I mean, I was going to . . . but I changed my mind."

"Give me standing room."

"Excuse me," said a teenage girl at Yale's window. "Do you know if that guy who plays Corky has a girlfriend?"

"How long did you wait in line to ask me that, you poor creature?"

"I'm sorry, sir," I told my customer. "Fire laws forbid standing room at our theater."

"Um . . . like, two hours?" the teenage girl told Yale.

"We can sit in the damn lighting booth, and I'll pay five hundred dollars a ticket."

"Hey, buddy, there's people behind you!"

And so it went, for two hours at least, until Roland mercifully put the CLOSED FOR A MOMENT sign in the window and gave us all a forty-five-minute lunch break. God, how I hated *Shakespearean Idol*.

By the time that break finally took place, I'd lost all interest in telling Yale about my day and was dead set on somehow making sense of it.

"Can I borrow your cell phone?" I said to him.

"I'm getting you your own for Christmas," Yale said, like he always did.

I took his phone and walked out of the theater as the rest of my coworkers stepped into the small courtyard to smoke cigarettes and eat and Roland—ever spry and springy for seventy-five—ran upstairs to report the day's initial take to the artistic director.

Giving us all a break at the same time instead of staggering us was a holdover from The Space's days of having no customers whatsoever. It might not have been terribly efficient, but Roland thought it was good for morale—the "forty-five minute vacation" he called it—and astonishingly, the fans in line never complained. They just sat on the sidewalk and picnicked 'til we returned. As if we were Shakespeare in the Park.

"I've got an idea," En told Shell. "You can eat one end of a protein bar, and I'll eat the other, and we'll meet in the middle. . . . You know what I'm saying?"

Yale said, "That's an exit cue if I ever heard one," and headed for the theater, where he now spent most of his downtime rehearsing for an upcoming audition at the Brooklyn Academy of Music to understudy KoKo in *The Mikado*.

It was his dream role—the Lord High Executioner, who couldn't bear the thought of killing another person. Knowing this, Roland had talked the artistic director into letting Yale use the stage whenever it was empty. Sometimes, he would show up as early as dawn to stand on that *Idol* set, with its balcony made out of gold records and microphones, and rehearse KoKo's big number—the one about laying your head on a block and waiting for the "short, sharp chop" of death.

A stabbed and mutilated woman. My age, my old apartment building. Why couldn't he have just told me?

"Sam!" Yale said, just before he entered the theater. "You're going to tell John about the new note, right?"

"Actually, there's something more important than that."

When I reached the end of the block, I flipped Yale's phone open and tapped in Krull's cell number.

"John Krull," he said, just like always.

"Why didn't you tell me?" I hadn't meant for the words to come out like that, so hard and accusatory.

No reply—just seconds of silence, with my question sitting there like a pile of broken glass. "I mean—"

"Tell you what?"

"Jesus, John."

"What is this, some kind of guessing game?"

Now it's his turn to accuse. When did we start having conversations like this? I took a deep breath. "Marla Soble. I heard it on the news."

More silence. Then, "Oh."

I closed my eyes. "That's why, right? You're upset because she lived in my old building? I need you to tell me these things. I need you to explain why—"

"Apartment."

"What?"

"She lived in your old apartment. She was killed in your apartment."

"She was—"

"You asked, so I'm telling you. I didn't tell you previously because I didn't think you wanted to know that someone went into your old apartment and lost control and stabbed a woman to death and, even though her dog howled all night, no one called the cops. I thought telling you that . . . *explaining* that to you . . . might hurt you more than my being a little uncommunicative, but—"

"I'm sorry."

"I guess I was wrong about what makes you upset. I guess—"

"I said I'm sorry." On the street, a cab blared its horn so loud I couldn't hear my own voice.

Krull said something.

"What?" I said.

". . . take it . . ."

"What?"

"I didn't mean to take it out on you. It's just been . . ."

"A difficult time?"

"Yeah."

"I understand."

"I'll see you tonight. Love you."

"You're not having an affair, are you?" I said. But he'd already hung up.

I pulled the note out of my back pocket and stared at the words. DON'T SHOW THIS TO HIM!!!!!

Was it really that important? As important as a

dog, alone in an apartment, smelling nothing but the spilled blood of its owner?

My old apartment. I remembered the way it looked the day I moved out. The dark parquet floors, the small window overlooking the air-shaft, the one wall of exposed brick that had seemed so New York to me, cold though it got in the wintertime. And the other three walls, clean and off-white, two tiny pinholes where I'd hung the framed Lichtenstein print I'd bought from the Museum of Modern Art the day I'd left Nate—a comic-book portrait of a dewy-eyed girl singing into a microphone.

I wondered if Marla had hung another picture in the same spot, if she had used the same pin-holes. I wondered which corner of the apartment was her dog's favorite, if she had dust bunnies under her couch like I did. I wondered if her blood had pooled on the parquet wood, if it had spattered the exposed brick.

"I guess I was wrong about what makes you upset."

I read the phone number at the bottom of the strange man's note, then pushed the buttons on Yale's cell phone. For a while I stared at the eleven digits across the tiny screen, thinking, *Who are you? What do you want to tell me?*

On the day I'd moved into his apartment, Krull had unwrapped the Lichtenstein print, and to-gether we'd hung it over his bed. Then we'd stood across the room, admiring the singing girl like proud parents.

"I like it there," he said.

"Me too."

"I like you here."

"Me too."

Reverie. That was the name of the print. It was still over our bed.

I hit SEND. Listened to it ring once, twice, three times. I was just about to forget the whole thing and hang up when I heard his voice—"Hello?"—lips tightening elegantly around the O. Where did he come from, anyway?

"It's Samantha."

"You found my new note?"

Found? Well, English is his second language.

"Hello?"

"Yes. I . . . I read it."

"Is he with you?"

"Who?" I said. "Is who with me? Who are you talking about?"

"I don't know his name. But he's planning . . ."

A bulky group of jocks, probably college guys, passed and one of them broadsided me, practically knocking me to the ground. "Sorry, ma'am," he said, but I didn't reply, didn't even look at him.

"Planning what?"

What followed was several seconds of silence, with both of us pressed to our phones. Over all the traffic noise, all the pedestrian chatter and car horns and trucks barreling by like giant waves, I swore I could hear this stranger breathing. Finally, he said, "I can't talk to you now. It's not safe."

"Just tell me—"

It came out a choked whisper, but still I could hear every word. "He is watching you."

"Right now?"

"Always."

I heard a click and a dial tone. And for a while, all I could do was stand there, remembering that feeling I'd had while talking on the pay phone, feeling it again like a stronger dose of the same, dizzying medicine.

As I walked back to the box office, I crossed my arms over my chest, tried to ignore the prickly heat at the base of my neck, the burning of unseen eyes up and down my spine. Instead, I focused all my attention on the sidewalk, carefully avoiding cracks and lines as if suddenly my life depended on it.

4

A Winner's Tale

Back at the box office, I begged Roland to switch me with En. Yale frowned, but I told him I'd explain later—I just couldn't work the window anymore.

Believe me, when you feel as though you're being watched, the last place you want to be is sitting in a ticket window. So I suffered through four hours of answering phones next to Shell Clarion and her dehydrated protein bars, three of which I'd eaten just to get her to stop saying, "gluten-free."

Bland as they seemed at first, the protein bars had a creeping, bitter aftertaste and as the day progressed, I felt as if I'd consumed a box of chalk. At least it was a Monday. Since the theater was dark, work lasted only until six p.m. rather than eight.

I grabbed my bag and quickly said good-bye to Shell, but the minute I stepped into the ticket room, my exhaustion evaporated and my heart started to pound.

"You look like you could use a little gluten," said Yale.

"Walk me home."

"I have to rehearse, hon. The audition's next week, and—"

"Please."

He looked at me. "Okay . . ."

As we walked, I told Yale how I'd called the stranger. I told him what he'd said, how I could actually *feel* the fear in the man's voice when he'd whispered, "He's watching you."

Yale didn't say anything right away; he just stared straight ahead.

"Don't tell me you still think he's a club promoter."

"Oh, Sam . . . of course not, but . . ."

"But what?"

"Do you feel like we're being watched right now?"

"Do you?"

"No. But you should trust your intuition, not mine. Yours is better."

I exhaled. "I felt like I was being watched

before work, when I was at a pay phone, leaving a message for my mother," I said. "After that, I went to see Krull, and he had this look on his face like he was getting ready to leave me. And then I found out there was a woman killed in my old apartment, and then I talked to this . . . person. So—"

"There was a woman killed in your old apartment?"

"Yeah, and her body was dumped in Washington Square Park, of all places. Somebody must have done it during the thunderstorm, because otherwise he would've had at least a hundred drunk NYU students as eyewitnesses."

"My God . . ."

"Yeah . . . so . . . I definitely feel like I'm going to jump out of my own skin, but whether or not it's because someone is watching me is up for debate."

"You want my advice? Don't call this asshole anymore."

"You don't think he was warning—"

Yale stopped me in the middle of the sidewalk, putting both hands on my shoulders. "I think . . . you've got a fan." He said it as if he were telling me I had a terminal illness. "I'm sure he's probably harmless—most of them are. But . . . you know. You don't want to encourage him."

"Why would I have a fan, Yale? I work two minimum-wage jobs. I live in Stuy Town."

"The *Post* called you a hero. The mayor gave you a fucking medal."

"That was a billion years ago. There's been a hell of a lot bigger heroes since then, and you know it."

"Well, this guy remembers you. My guess is, he's trying to get you scared again, so you run to him for help, and *he* becomes *your* hero. Come on—he tells Veronica your first and last name, but he can't even give you the initials of this man who's supposedly watching you always and has some sort of plan that he knows of—and didn't tell you about, by the way?"

I looked at him. "You've got a point."

"Of course I do. I know what makes people tick—especially fans." He started walking again. "Don't tell Peter, but . . . when I was ten, I used to daydream about setting Rob Lowe's house on fire and then saving him from it."

I widened my eyes at him.

"Come on, I never *did* anything about it."

We were almost at Stuyvesant Town. The sky was going glowing, gaudy pink as the sun set behind our backs. *Home before dark,* I thought. But still I felt that awful tingling at the base of my skull, down my neck, across my shoulders. *He can see you better in daylight.* "Can I ask you some-thing, Yale?"

"I saw Rob Lowe's house *once.* I was in a damn tour bus with my parents and my sister and I never went anywhere near—"

"Not that," I said. "Do you . . . feel like we're being watched right now?"

"No, honey, I still don't." Yale grabbed my hand and squeezed it, and didn't let go until we were in front of my apartment building. Just before he left, Yale said, "There's no way in hell John would ever leave you. Why would you think that?"

Because last night, after lying in bed alone for three hours, I said out loud, "He's gone for good." And the only thing that made me think I might be wrong was that he hadn't taken the cat.

I didn't say that to Yale, though, because I didn't tell him things like that. Didn't tell anyone things like that. I'd always believed that once you start talking behind your lover's back, the rela-tionship's done. "He just looked kind of . . . cold," I said. "I mean . . . you know . . . for him."

"Trust me," said Yale. "He'd rather die than leave you. He winked. "I know what makes peo-ple tick."

When I opened the door to my apartment, the first thing I heard was a man's voice shouting, "I'm gonna kill that fuckin' bitch!"

I gasped, but only because I was startled. I'd walked in on enough similar outbursts to recognize it was only Pierce, yelling at a Yankees game.

I dropped my purse by the door and went into the living room where, sure enough, Krull and Pierce were sitting at opposite ends of the couch in front of the TV, a large pepperoni pizza on the coffee table. Jake the cat was lying on his back on Krull's lap, grasping a pizza crust between his paws, while biting into it enthusiastically. He reminded me of a stoned, fat jazz musician playing the clarinet, and I have to say, I admired his complete lack of self-consciousness—his trust that the lap would never go away.

"Strange cat you got there," Pierce told Krull.

"He likes crusts," I said.

"Hi, Sam. I didn't hear you come in."

Krull smiled up at me. "Missed you," he said.

Then what was this afternoon about? "Me, too."

"Zach brought beer if you want some. It's in the fridge."

"Thanks." I went into the kitchen and came back with a cold, sweaty can.

This wasn't how I'd expected to spend the evening, but in a way it was better. Much as Krull and I needed to talk, I didn't want to. Maybe his reluctance to discuss problems had finally rubbed off on me, but the thought of having a beer while

listening to Pierce overreact to baseball plays
sounded a lot more appealing.

Krull slid closer to Pierce, making room for me
at the end of the couch. I squeezed in beside him
and scratched Jake's tummy. "So Zachary, who
exactly was it you wanted to kill?" I asked.

"Jeter. They pay him too much. He's getting so
soft it's . . . I'm sorry, Sam. I wouldn't have called
him a B if I knew you were here."

"No offense taken. I'm a Dodgers fan."

"You're shitting me."

"Sadly, no," said Krull. "Her grandmother
brainwashed her when she was a kid."

I stared straight ahead, making my voice into a
robotic monotone: "TheYankeesareastorebought-
team."

Pierce chuckled.

Krull put his arm around my back and rubbed
my bare shoulder. Maybe talking things out was
overrated, after all. Because no matter what he
might have said about where he was last night or
why he'd been so quiet, there was nothing so re-
assuring as the gentle way in which he touched
my shoulder.

"Did you see that? He just stole third! I swear
to God, Steinbrenner needs to fire every one of
those fuckin' women, starting with Wells."

Krull turned to me. "How was the first day of
school?"

"Fine."

"Didn't they like making the collages?"

"I used to love making collages when I was a kid," said Pierce. "It was the one kind of art I could do."

"These are called 'All About Me' collages," Krull said. "A nice way for the kids to introduce themselves, but our closet was like a magazine re-cycling bin all summer, right, Sam?"

"You'll be happy to know they used almost every issue."

"Did you have *Playboy*?" said Pierce.

Krull sighed. "No, Zach, she didn't get *Playboy* for the four-year-olds."

"Because if I was going to make an 'All About Me' collage, I'd need *Playboy*," he said. Then, "*Fucking Wells!*" At the top of his lungs, without warning. Like some kind of testosterone bomb, detonating in the middle of our apartment.

Jake thudded to the floor and scurried out of the room.

"Jesus," Krull said. "It was only ball one."

"You mind if we turn off the TV for a couple of minutes?" Pierce said. "I just need a little . . . per-spective."

"I think that's an excellent idea." I flicked off the power button, though Krull rolled his eyes. The situation reminded me of something I might encounter in the classroom. *It's not fair, Ms. Leiffer.*

Just 'cause Zachary needs a time-out, how come we all have to get punished?

"Take a few deep breaths and find your center, Zach," Krull said. "Repeat after me. 'It's only a game. It's only—'"

"Okay, okay," Pierce said. "I get the point."

I bit into a piece of lukewarm pizza, took a sip of my beer. "Anyway, what I was going to say about my class was, I had to break up two fights today."

"That seems excessive," Krull said.

"Tell me about it. And one of them involved glue. My poor green shirt will never be the same."

"Boys will be boys," Pierce said.

Krull looked at him. "Why would you say that?"

Pierce shrugged his shoulders. "It's part of being a kid, right? You get into fights."

"But Sam never said it was boys who were fighting."

"Oh . . . I . . . I just assumed that—"

"Girls fight too, you know. Just because a kid's a boy, it doesn't mean he's some sort of violent personality, who—"

"Actually, both fights were coed," I said.

Pierce's face was starting to flush.

I glared at Krull. "But I think it's perfectly reasonable to assume I was talking about boys."

"Not if you're a detective."

Pierce's face darkened another shade. His head drooped like a shamed dog.

Christ, John, what is your problem? I forced a smile. "As a preschool teacher I can tell you with *certainty* that boys are more prone to physical violence."

Krull said, "Really?"

Pierce gave him a glare so hard and cold I half expected bullets to shoot out of his eyes. "That was a man who did that to her," he said. "A man who was good and pissed off, and you know it."

"I don't know anything. And you know less."

"What are you guys talking about?" I said.

"Marla Soble," said Pierce. "Both our units caught the case, and we're working with these guys from the Tenth and everyone—fucking everyone—agrees her fiancé is a major person of interest, except your boyfriend here. She cheated on him, for chrissakes."

"I don't want to talk about it."

"You're the one who brought it up!"

"No, I didn't. I was talking about boys. Little boys from Sam's class, you asshole—"

"Hey, calm down." Pierce shot him a look. "Find your *fucking center*, why don't you."

Several seconds passed, during which the only sound came from Jake, who was such a noisy eater you could hear him crunching his food all the way in the kitchen. He made another sound too, like the smacking of lips, which still freaked me out.

Shortly after I'd moved in, I'd mentioned that smacking sound to Krull, in bed. "Cats don't have lips," he'd replied.

An odd statement to begin with, but hilarious to two people in the giddy aftermath of sex. Krull and I had lain on our backs, laughing until tears trickled into our hair and our breath came out in gasps.

"He's at it again," I said.

Krull said, "Who?"

"The lip-smacker."

"Oh. Right."

I looked at Pierce. "Our cat smacks his lips when he eats."

"Ah . . . weird cat. Listen, John. I—"

"I'm gonna get another beer," said Krull. "Either of you guys want one?"

"Sure," Pierce said.

After Krull left for the kitchen, Pierce edged closer to me on the couch. "He's taking this case too personally."

"Well . . . I used to live in that apartment."

"I know that," he said. "But I don't think that's the reason. There's something else going on in his head about Soble. Something he can relate to, or . . ."

"Yeah?"

"Maybe it's the cheating part."

I stared at him.

"I'm kidding, Sam," he said, but I didn't laugh. Didn't even smile.

As soon as Krull came back from the kitchen, I turned the game back on, and the evening elapsed without incident. The Yankees even won, adding credence to Pierce's belief that screaming obscenities at a TV screen in Stuyvesant Town can affect the outcome of a baseball game at a stadium ten miles away. No mention was made of the Soble case—not even peripherally—until the very end of the evening. After the postgame show was over, Pierce said, "Well, I'm ready to call it a night. Can I take a few slices home for the ghost?"

As I went into the kitchen to wrap three pieces of pizza in tinfoil, I heard Krull say to Pierce, "Sorry about what happened earlier. I . . . just have a lot on my mind."

"No worries," he replied.

Speak for yourself.

After Pierce took his slices and left, I started stacking up the plates and empty beer cans to bring into the kitchen.

"I'll clean up," Krull said. "You should relax. You've had a tough day."

For the first time since I'd come home, I remembered my phone conversation with the stranger from Starbucks. I was sure Yale was right—I was dealing with a low-aiming obsessed fan who realized it was easier to get responses from Good Samaritans than from movie stars. Why had I called him, anyway?

Right now, what he'd said to me seemed irrelevant—even a little embarrassing, like those obscene calls I used to get when my full first name was listed in the book. *"Hi, Samantha. Are you naked right now?"*

"My day hasn't been that tough," I said.

"Two fights? One involving a poisonous substance? That's more action than I've seen, and I'm the cop."

I smiled.

"Sit on the couch. Read. I got you that *New Yorker* on my way home from work." He grabbed the magazine from atop the dinette near the window, and handed it to me.

"I forgot about that," I said. There was supposedly an item in the "Talk of the Town" column about the block-long ticket lines for *Shakespearean Idol.* Roland had even been interviewed for it— the first and last time the Space would make the *New Yorker,* I was certain.

I opened the magazine as Krull took the plates into the kitchen, and turned to "Talk of the

Town." Sure enough, the *Shakespearean Idol* piece, "A Winner's Tale," was right up front, following an editorial about the upcoming September 11 anniversary, titled, "Are We Any Safer?"

"Did you read this?" I said.

"Didn't get a chance," Krull called out from the kitchen. "Pierce was waiting outside the door when I got home." After a short pause, he said, "Can I ask you something?"

"Yes, I do, but he'll get over it."

Krull walked back into the room. "Huh?"

"Weren't you going to ask me if I thought you were too hard on Zachary?"

"No."

"Oh," I said. "I guess I'm still not psychic, huh?"

"I was going to ask if you meant what you said about boys—men—being naturally more violent?"

"Well . . . yeah, of course."

"Look at me, Sam. I'm a man." I glanced up at him. His eyes locked onto mine, as if he were offering me some sort of challenge. "Do you think violence is a part of my DNA?"

"If it is," I said slowly, "you're obviously able to fight against it."

He sat next to me on the couch.

I heard myself say, "You know what else is supposed to be hardwired into male DNA?"

"What?"

"The urge to sleep with many different women

in order to propagate the species." I stared into his eyes. "You fight against that, don't you?"

He moved a little closer.

"Don't you?"

Krull kissed me gently on the mouth. It was like a sip of cold water after a long, draining run, and I wanted more. I wanted the whole bottle. "What urges do women have?" he said.

"Well." I kissed his face, trailed my fingers through his thick, clean hair. "There's the urge to get pregnant."

"That's a pretty serious urge." Krull's voice hummed into the back of my neck, spreading a tingling warmth throughout my body, and as he scooped me up in his arms and carried me into the bedroom, I thought, *You never answered my previous question, but who gives a damn?*

We made love like two people who would never leave each other.

"A Winner's Tale" started out with an anecdote about a nineteen-year-old girl from New Jersey who had seen the show a hundred times. I had met this girl, of course—sold her at least fifty of those tickets. Her name was Tabitha Meeks, and she was big and chesty, with dyed black hair and an entire wardrobe of billowing black gauze. She spoke very softly for someone so large, and her clothes seemed not so much a fashion statement as an effort to disappear, to fade into the darkness of the theater once the houselights went down.

But in this article, which I read in bed while Krull finished in the kitchen, she came across as a different person—the media-savvy doppelgänger of the Tabitha I knew. She repeatedly called the reporter *honeychild* (as in, "Honeychild, I sniffed this show out as a hit from day one!"), used expressions like *boffo* and claimed a "special friendship" with Corky, Juliana and the whole "*SI* family."

While the accompanying illustration was a caricature of Corky, belting out a number in front of an arm-waving throng, Tabitha was the article's true star. "Ms. Meeks opens her pocketbook and produces a bumper sticker she's made herself," the last paragraph read. "In hot-pink letters against a solid-gold background is the slogan she calls the 'Keep on Truckin'' of the new millennium: 'Corky and Juliana: 'Til Death.'"

"Unbelievable."

"What's unbelievable?" said Krull, who had a way of sneaking into rooms so quietly, it was almost as if he'd materialized out of nowhere. It was a habit he'd picked up as a uniformed cop, sneaking into meth labs, and it never failed to give me palpitations.

"Jeez, ninja lawman, try clearing your throat sometime."

"Sorry." He was standing over me wearing his boxers and a gray NYPD T-shirt spattered with sink water. I thought about him the previous night, absent for hours and then wet from the rain.

I exhaled. "This fan from the theater, Tabitha? She's in this article and she sounds so . . . different."

"Maybe she was misquoted."

"The *New Yorker* would never misquote someone," I said. "Especially someone saying things like *honeychild* and *boffo*. That's grounds for a lawsuit."

Krull shrugged his shoulders, then pulled off his shirt. "Maybe you don't know this fan as well as you thought you did."

I looked at him. "Maybe not."

He slipped into bed beside me. "Are you still reading or do you mind if I turn off the light?"

"You can turn it off. . . . John?"

"Mmm-hmm?"

Where were you last night? Ask now. It's easier in the dark. "Where . . . Was Marla really cheating on her fiancé?"

The question hung in the room for what seemed like an unnaturally long time. I listened to the hum of the air conditioner, wondering if Krull hadn't fallen asleep, until finally, he said, "I don't know."

"Well, it sounded like everyone—"

"She kept a journal," said Krull. "And . . . I'm sorry, Sam. I really don't want to talk about her. I can't."

I heard a crash in the living room and jumped a little, even though I knew it was only the massive cat, landing on the floor. Predictably, the thump of his paws moved closer and closer to our room, like something out of a monster movie. "He's late," I said.

"I gave him more pizza crust when I was cleaning up. He must've just finished."

When he reached our bed, Jake jumped up on the sheet covering my stomach and knocked the breath out of me.

Then he stood up and began to knead the area with all four paws—something cats supposedly do when they've been separated from their mothers too early.

Jake did this deliberately enough so that his needly claws pierced the sheet and dug into my skin. This was something of a nightly ritual, but that didn't make it any less irritating. Sydney— who wasn't above analyzing anyone, even a cat—had become claw fodder herself during a visit the previous year, and determined it was "an orphan's revenge against female authority figures."

Finally, Jake completed the ritual and collapsed.

I gasped. "You might want to ease up on the pizza crusts."

Krull said, "He's just big boned."

"Like a woolly mammoth is big boned."

"I love you, you know."

I turned my head, watched his face. He was staring at the ceiling in a way that reminded me of someone floating on his back in the middle of the ocean, looking up at the night sky. Who knew what lurked in the deep water beneath him, or when it would rise up to the surface? He was comfortable now, and for him, that was enough.

"I love you, too," I said.

I was starting to fall asleep when I heard the slam of a door and a shrill female voice: ". . . the fuck have you been?!"

Our neighbors. Krull and I had such a strange relationship with these people. We'd never seen them—they entered the building through the east entrance, while we used the west. We didn't know their names or how old they were. But thanks to the thin wall between our apartment and theirs, we knew their most intimate secrets. We didn't know what he did for a living, but we knew she suspected him of cheating on her with the receptionist at his office. We had no idea what she looked like, but we knew she drank enough to ruin her face. We knew they had no children. We knew it was his fault she couldn't get pregnant.

This couple fought almost every night at midnight. When I'd first moved in, Krull had told me you could set a watch by them. I looked at the digital clock on my nightstand. Twelve o'clock. *They never fail.*

"You were with *her*, weren't you? Don't try to lie, you fuck!"

She could break glass with that voice. Was that why I couldn't ask Krull where he'd been last night—because I was afraid of sounding like her?

". . . off my back, you churchin' bitch!" Churching? He must have said something else. Turgid? Merchant? He was often hard to hear, unlike his wife, who was clear as a local radio signal.

I want to say the arguing bothered me. It's what I told Krull, what I told all my friends. But the truth was, I found it fascinating. And that's what really bothered me—not the fighting, but the way I reacted to it.

"You know what you are?" she shrieked. "A goddamn sympathy vulture!"

She's quoting my mother. I almost started to laugh, until I heard a meaty clap . . . skin hitting skin. I'd never heard that sound out of them before. My breath caught in my throat.

"Aaaahhh . . ." *Call the police. But it was just one*

slap. One sob. Do I need to get involved? They'd probably get mad. Maybe she slapped herself.

"You hurt me!"

Then a crash, and my mind went to my old apartment, the four dead bolts on the door, the thin wall behind the pullout couch.

What did Marla's neighbors hear?

"Get away . . ."

Call the police.

". . . gonna kill you!"

Did she say anything to her killer? Did anyone hear her, begging for her life?

I started to get out of bed, but then he said something—I couldn't tell what. He was saying it softly, though. Was he apologizing? Or was it a threat? Who knew? Who even knew what their apartment number was?

"Go to hell, you fat, sterile motherfucker," she said, clear as ever. *Okay, she's fine.*

I put my head on Krull's chest, listening to them yelling at each other, just like always, until I fell back to sleep.

Just as I was drifting off, the thought came to me again. *What did Marla's neighbors hear?* But this time I knew the answer, and with that absolute certainty you feel only when you're not conscious enough to move, let alone doubt. The answer was this: *The neighbors didn't hear anything. She died before making a sound.*

5

Bloody Valentine

He was shirtless, with the smooth, pale musculature of an Italian statue. He wore tight black jeans, and his hair was black, too, but I couldn't see his face, because I was following him through the lobby of a building, into an elevator—both of which were so full of blossoming plants it was difficult to move. The blooms looked fake. They glowed like neon.

The elevator went up, up, up. He plucked a flower from one of the plants and handed it to me. It was black and fist shaped, and when I looked at it, it crumbled. "It's called a Marla," he said. "Isn't it beautiful?"

The elevator door opened, and I kept following him down a long, narrow hallway until he stopped at a door: twelve-B.

"Check this out." He spun around. He had no face, but I had only a second to register this before the apartment door flew open and we were both hit with a torrent of blood.

I opened my eyes fast on the nightstand clock blinking seven a.m. It took me a few panicky seconds to verify where I was, and that I'd been dreaming. I stretched out, but all I felt next to me was Jake, who, as it turned out, was sprawled across my boyfriend's vacated pillow. *Where did he go now?*

I sat up in bed and saw Krull, fully dressed for work in a beige suit coat and pants, hunched over the closet safe. But rather than taking his gun out to wear to work, he seemed to be putting something away. Interesting. I watched him closing the small door and spinning the lock.

"Hiding a present from me?" I said.

He spun around fast, just like the faceless man in my dream. "You scared me."

I stretched. "What are you doing up so early?"

"Well," he said, "I woke up at six and couldn't sleep, so I went out. Did some shopping."

From the floor next to the safe, he produced a swirl of green tissue paper, and I knew what was inside before he handed it to me. Three Sterling roses.

"One for 'I,' one for 'love' and one for 'you,'" Krull said.

I put the lavender flowers up to my face, inhaling deeply. "My favorites." Sterling roses had been my favorite for a long time—ever since my grandmother gave me a bouquet of them as a thirteenth birthday present. "They're like you," she'd said, pointing to blooms a color you'd never expect from a rose. "Surprising."

Krull said, "I don't know why you couldn't like red or white or yellow roses instead. I had to go to four different florists to find these."

I grinned at him. "I appreciate the effort."

"There's bagels in the kitchen, too. And I made coffee, and put food out for Jake."

"To what do I owe all this?" *Do you feel guilty for cheating on me two nights ago?*

"To me having too much time on my hands." He sat on the edge of the bed. "Listen, I don't want to freak you out."

My spine straightened a little. "Usually when you say something like that, it's sort of like a backhanded prophecy."

"I know." Krull took a deep breath. "This probably isn't anything at all, but . . ."

"What, John?"

"Louise, at the newsstand? She . . . says hi, by the way."

I just stared at him.

"Okay . . . Louise said she thought she might have heard your mother might be moving to New

York. Just for a short time . . . for some radio thing."

"Oh, my God it's actually true?"

"She didn't know for sure—a friend had mentioned it. Come to think of it, I bet she heard it from Pierce. He goes to that newsstand all the time."

"Really? You're not just saying that to—"

"Your mother would call you if she were coming out here, Sam. She's not that much of a bitch. I just wanted to give you a heads-up, in case Louise says something to you about it."

"Ummm . . . thanks."

He kissed me. "I gotta go."

"But it's so early."

"Press conference," he said.

"Marla?"

"Yeah . . . How's the suit?"

I smiled at him. The fact that he looked great in head-to-toe beige polyester said a lot more about his body—or at least, how I felt about his body— than it did about what happened to be covering it. "It's perfect," I said. "Good luck."

Marla Soble's picture was on the cover of that day's *Post* and the *Daily News.* I bought both on my way to Sunny Side, staring at her face as I handed quarters to Louise.

"Would you look at that," said Louise. "A 1947 quarter. Know what I was doing in 1947?"

"Being born?"

"Getting *divorced,* you sweet, wonderful girl."

I couldn't take my eyes off Marla's face.

"You know, Sam, she looks a little like you," said Louise. "I mean . . . looked. Poor thing."

Both newspapers had chosen the same cover picture—smiling, dark-haired, vaguely Semitic Marla, her arm thrown around the neck of a large golden retriever. They were on a beach together and the sun made halos around their heads. According to the captions, the dog's name was Lucky.

Who took this photo? Who told the papers Lucky's name?

Marla had soulful brown eyes like her dog, a glowing tan that looked like it came from the sun, not a salon. She probably bicycled everywhere, didn't need caffeine in the morning, ate three healthy meals a day. She had another sixty years ahead of her, at least.

"They think her fiancé did it," Louise said.

"Who told you that, Zachary Pierce?"

"How did you know?"

"Just a guess."

"Fatal Attraction?" asked the *Daily News* headline. But the *Post's* was more specific: "Her Killer Left a Bloody Valentine."

I opened the paper and skimmed the printed columns for an explanation until I noticed the black-and-white photograph in the lower right-hand corner of the spread.

It was the outline of a large heart, drawn in dripping blood on an exposed brick wall.

I gasped. "Jesus."

"And they call themselves a fuckin' family newspaper," said Louise.

"I used to live there, Louise," I said. "In that apartment."

"Shit . . . I didn't know that. John didn't tell me—"

"I . . . I put my dinette set in front of that wall, so when I drank my coffee in the morning, I'd feel like I was in a downtown café."

"Honey, I'm sorry."

"When I moved out, I . . ." *I said to Krull, "That wall is the one thing I'll miss about this place."*

"You what, honey?"

"Nothing." *Why didn't he tell me? He must've known.* "Who would do something like this?"

"A very sick, very angry motherfucker," Louise said, and as she said it my eyes went to the picture on the following page—the picture of Marla and her fiancé, a slim, bespectacled NYU photography professor named Gil Valdez who looked neither sick nor angry.

"Wait 'til you're my age," she said. "You'll have four dead bolts on your door, and you won't trust anybody."

Marla had five. Three dead bolts seemed like too few, and I'd wanted an odd number for good luck.

Louise said, "Didn't mean to make a big deal out of my age like that. You probably think I'm a sympathy vulture."

I smiled a little. "Never."

She came out from behind the counter and gave me a quick hug. Her skin was dry and cool and smelled of flour. If I closed my eyes, it was exactly like hugging my grandmother. "Take good care of that man of yours," she said. "We need him around to protect us."

I arrived at Sunny Side to find Veronica standing in front of my classroom. "Hi," I said.

She held something out to me—a small, sealed red envelope. *Another note? Does this guy ever give up?*

I took the envelope from Veronica, and when I looked at the pattern that had been embossed into it, my breath suddenly got shallow. Dozens and dozens of Valentine hearts. "I . . . don't want to open this."

"Aren't you curious?"

"Of course not."

"Can I have it then?"

I squinted at her. Why in a million years would she want a note from someone else's stalker?

Her cheeks went inexplicably pink. "Never mind." She began to move away, but I grabbed her arm.

"What the hell is wrong with you?"

"No need to get all cussy."

"Well, come on," I said. "You yourself said you thought he was lascivious and up to no good, and—"

"Oh, no, no, no." She started laughing, which, as far as I was concerned, was the whipped cream and cherry on top of a banana split of bizarre behavior.

"Uh . . . Veronica?"

Finally she caught her breath enough to speak. "It's not from that Arabian fellow. It's from Nate Gundersen."

I grimaced.

"He said he had an early call at the studio and just wanted to stop by. I love the way these actors talk, with their early calls. It's so glamorous, don't you think?"

I turned the envelope over and noticed silver cursive words nestled among the hearts. *Nate Gundersen Fan Club.*

As I opened it, Veronica kept talking, her voice higher and faster, as if she had just sucked up a dose of helium or had suddenly reverted to puberty. "He was really so nice, and I know that was silly of me to ask for the note, but my mother, she's a huge *Live and Let Live* fan, and Lucas is her favorite character. . . ."

Inside, matching red stationery with more of those cursed hearts. The initials NGFC, again in silver, were positioned in the top left-hand corner, where the return address should be.

"I thought I could just snip out the part where he signed the note, if it's okay with you. . . ."

I started to read:

> *Dear Samantha,*
> *Please come see me. I need to talk to you.*
> *XO, Nate*

Folded up in the red paper was an official studio pass, admitting me onto the *Live and Let Live* set on West Seventy-seventh Street.

Every housewife's dream.

I ripped *XO, Nate* from the note and gave it to Veronica, along with the pass. "Tell your mom to knock herself out."

"Oh, thank you, thank you, Samantha!"

As soon as I got into my classroom, I threw the rest of Nate's note in the trash and yelled, "Leave me alone!" at it.

Okay, focus. You've got a class to prepare for. I fished around in my stuffed purse for the key to the art supplies closet. I felt my box-office keys, my apartment keys, my classroom keys, the keys to Yale and Peter's new apartment on Twenty-eighth Street, my wallet, three boxes of crayons, the newspapers I'd bought from Louise, my half-read copy of *The Art of Caring*, a six-month-old pack of gum . . . and the triangular note. *I was going to throw this away. Didn't I?*

I put the note on top of the desk, while hearing Ezra's voice in my mind: *"Is that your fortune?"* But that thought was interrupted—not by actual movement or sound—but by a sudden slithering feeling.

I was being watched.

I glanced at the classroom door—shut. Then I crept toward the large, street-facing window, slow and tentative as a child sneaking up on a butterfly. *I know you're out there; I can feel your eyes. . . .*

I put my face right up to the window, making myself skim the clusters of people hurrying down the sidewalk. I searched the inching morning traffic, peered into the backseats of cabs. No one looked back.

Still . . .

I looked across the street at the Gap, at the headless mannequins in the window, lined up like the hearts on Nate's note—all of them in neon-colored tank tops, all of them stiff and white as corpses.

I could see part of the pay phone on the corner;

I let my eyes travel back down the street and up. Next to the Gap was a narrow five-story walk-up. In the second-floor window, someone—barely a shadow from this distance and through that thick, dirty window—was holding one of the curtains open.

I held up my hand and waved. The curtains swung shut.

Now who's paranoid?

At least the drapes were closed now. Whoever had been watching me had been scared enough to back away. I squinted up at the window, trying to discern a shadow behind the white cloth but, with no lights on in the apartment, that was impossible.

I shut my venetian blinds. It was best to be cautious. It was always best to be cautious.

But even with them shut, I couldn't get rid of the feeling that someone was watching me. Closely.

I kept the blinds shut most of the way through class, even though the theme of the day was "Things you see on the street."

"Miss Leiffer, how can I draw a stoplight when I can't see one?" said Abraham.

"Use your imagination."

"But there's a stoplight right outside the wind—"

"Don't draw a stoplight, then. Draw a sidewalk. Or a tree, or some pigeons or whatever else you can remember seeing on the street when you came to school. Do I have to explain everything to you guys? Do you always have to be so . . . so . . . literal?"

Abraham looked at me, a promise of tears seeping into his huge brown eyes, and I felt like a heel. An actual heel—the thickest part of the foot, capable of grinding small, fragile things into the ground. "I'm sorry, honey," I said. "Guess I had a little too much coffee this morning, huh?"

"My mom puts this cream on her legs to stop cellulife," said Ida. "And it's made out of coffee beans."

"What's cellulife?" Ezra asked her.

"It's lumpy things that grow under your skin when you grow up."

"Ewwwww," said at least three of the kids in unison, Abraham being one of them, and I was grateful, at least, that someone had broken the tension.

"How big do they grow?" said Charlotte.

"Big," said Ida. "My mom hates cellulife and so she vanquishes them with the cream."

"That's scary."

"Yeah. But—"

"I think my dad has that."

"Ewww!"

As subtly as a person could in front of eight

preschoolers, I walked up to the window, flattened myself against the wall and peered behind the blinds like a B-movie fugitive. I was thankful everyone was too busy talking about their parents' thighs to notice what I was doing, even when I shimmied down the wall in order to see the walk-up better.

"My mom doesn't have lumps on the tops of her legs," said Ezra.

Harry W. replied, "Bet she does."

"No, she doesn't. Stars don't have lumpy legs."

"Ezra's mommy has lumpy legs! Ezra's mommy has lumpy legs!"

I found the building and glanced up at the second-floor window. I saw the closed draperies, and I was about to head back for the front of the classroom when I noticed sunlight glinting off two tiny glass circles poking out between them. Binoculars.

I jumped away from the blinds.

Meanwhile, my class was starting to sound like a session of the Taiwanese parliament.

"My mom does not have bumps!" Ezra yelled.

"She does! She does! She does!" the Weiss twins chanted.

"No!"

"She's got bumps! She's got bumps!"

"She does not because she is a great big TV star and your mommy isn't so shut up!"

I came up fast behind Ezra and put a hand on his shoulder. *"That's enough!"*

My "voice of authority," as Yale called it. Practiced at home in front of the mirror and honed to back-straightening perfection over four years, it was guaranteed to suck the sound out of any preschool classroom in seconds—and it didn't fail me now. Even *I* was a little stunned.

"But Ms. Leiffer, I was just—"

"I said that's enough. No more talking about cellulite ever, anymore, for the rest of the year. Is that clear?"

Ezra nodded.

For the rest of this class, I would forget the freak across the street and his binoculars (*Looking at what? Venetian blinds?*). I would not think about valentine hearts—lined up on Nate's fan club stationary, scrawled in blood on an exposed brick wall. I would not be a receiver of vague warnings folded up into triangles. I would not be afraid.

"Okay, then," I said. "Can anybody name one thing they might see on a street?"

"A stoplight," said Abraham.

I drew a reasonable approximation of a traffic signal on the blackboard, using green, yellow and red chalk to make the circular lights.

"What else? Charlotte?"

"A girl walking a dog."

"You got it."

"Ezra."

"Ummm . . . a limo?"

"Beautiful."

I'd always been pretty good at drawing; now I felt like an artist. And the more confident I became, the faster and more detailed I got with the chalk. I drew everything the kids told me to draw—buildings, pigeons, cars, blooming window boxes, a group of stick-figure kids kicking a soccer ball. Suggestions flew at me.

"Draw Toys 'R' Us!" shouted Ida.

"Draw a basketball hoop!" Harry S. said.

"How about a hot-dog guy?"

"Garbage cans!"

"Fire truck! Fire truck!"

With every new class, I hoped for that one moment when I stopped being a stranger or even a teacher and started being a friend. It didn't always happen—never as early as the second day—but here it was, way ahead of schedule. *I could work birthday parties.*

If I hadn't been facing those closed venetian blinds, this would easily have been the highlight of my career.

"More birdies!"

"A policeman holding a kitty cat!"

"A boy with another dog, and the dog is going poop!"

"Yeah!"

When the suggestions stopped coming, we all sat there admiring the blackboard street . . . so crowded and colorful. So safe.

"I wish I lived there," said Charlotte.

"Me too," I said.

When parents started showing up, I knocked on Veronica's door and got one of her assistants to watch my class while I rushed to the pay phone and called Krull's cell phone. I got his voice mail, then phoned the Sixth Precinct and had him paged. Krull wasn't around—nobody knew where he was—so Gayle Cruz connected me with Amanda Patton instead. After I told her that someone had been spying on me from the second-story apartment across the street, she said she'd be right over, with her other partner, Art Boyle.

"You really think this is a two-person job?" I asked.

"Nah," she said. "Art just wants to check out that new Gap."

By the time I got back to my classroom, most of the kids had left already—save Ida, who was loudly protesting her mother's plans for the rest of her day ("I'm not going to violin lessons and you can't make me!") and Ezra, still in the same chair, paging through the class's worn, five-year-old copy of *The Runaway Bunny.*

"Ezra," I said. "Is your nanny supposed to pick you up again today?"

"Mommy's getting me. We're gonna see the new IMAX picture."

"That sounds like fun."

Finally, Ida and her exhausted-looking mother reached a compromise involving mint-chocolate-chip ice cream.

And since Veronica's aide had long ago returned to her classroom, that left only Ezra and me. I watched him, gazing at the picture of Mommy Bunny as wind, blowing her sailboat baby to safety. *Should I call your mom?* I wanted to say. But I knew better. It sucked to be the one kid left waiting—the kid whose mother had better things to do than pick him up on time. I knew, because I had been that kid.

In seventh grade, I'd waited in the school parking lot for three hours because Sydney had agreed to do a last-minute talk-show appearance without making any other arrangements.

It wasn't the first time something like that had happened, but it was the worst. I could still remember sitting on that splintery bench, saying good-bye to my friends one by one, acting as if nothing were wrong and hating . . . not my mother, but my dad. For leaving me with her.

"You sure you don't want a ride?" said Jessica, my lab partner from biology class. "It's really getting late."

"No, my mom's coming. She just had to . . . pick up some groceries."

Teachers started leaving. Then the janitor.

When Sydney finally arrived, I was long past anger. The sun was beginning to set, and I fell into her arms weeping, just because she was alive. "Oh, honey," she said as she held me. "What's wrong?"

I watched Ezra, wondering if he hated his father, too. "*The Runaway Bunny* is one of my favorites. Would you like me to read it to you?"

He looked up from the book, raising his pale eyebrows in a way that made his face seem weirdly mature. I half expected him to say, *"Oh, pardon me! I thought you were talking to someone else."*

But what he actually said was, "My uncle Nate has sleepovers with my mom."

"That's nice." *Just keep him away from your nanny, and your dad and your dog and your goldfish.*

"Do you have sleepovers with him too?" Ezra asked.

I sighed. "We used to be friends, but it was a very, very long time ago. The last time I talked to your uncle Nate was before you were born."

"Sorry I'm late," said a voice behind me. I

turned and looked up at a tall, slender woman who could have been anywhere from twenty-five to forty-five years old. Jenna Sargent. Finally.

"I was just about to call you," I said.

"Well, here I am." Jenna's features were symmetrical and motionless, coated in a thick layer of what had to be her TV makeup. She wore dark pressed jeans, a white tank top and a red silk scarf, with matching chopsticks jammed into the golden chignon on top of her head. Her eyes were a rich, Caribbean blue, and her teeth were whiter than the mannequins in the window of the Gap. She said, "Do you always call parents when they're just half an hour late?"

"Well . . . yes, actually." *It's a preschool, not a cocktail party,* I wanted to say. But I stopped myself. I never argued with parents or guardians, because Terry always took their side.

But more than that, I was intimidated. Jenna Sargent wasn't so much beautiful as she was spotless, poreless—a perfect image peeled off a TV screen. I couldn't believe she was screwing a sex addict.

"I'd asked Soccoro to come," she said. "But apparently she didn't get my message."

How can she wear that much lipstick and not get it all over her teeth?

"Please don't let it happen again," I said. "Ezra

was here all by himself and we were worried. But . . . these things happen."

"I wasn't worried," said Ezra. "Mommy, can we go to IMAX now?"

Jenna was glaring into my trash can, at the crushed remnants of Nate's note. "I know that stationery," she said.

I shrugged. "Every day is Valentine's Day for Nate Gundersen fans."

She shifted her gaze from the trash can to me. "So," she said. "The famous Samantha Leiffer."

I was trying to figure out how to respond to that when Amanda Patton and Art Boyle showed up. They were a highly disparate pair—Patton impeccably dressed, especially for a cop, with her lean, aerobics-toned body and wholesome good looks; Boyle rumpled, meaty, florid. Krull seemed to balance them out, somehow. But with him missing, they turned into a sight gag.

"Hi, there, kiddo," Amanda said to Ezra. "You know, I have a son who's just about three years younger than you."

Jenna smirked. "And we're supposed to care about that because . . . ?"

"Sam, who is this nasty—"

"Jesus, Patton, don't you ever watch TV?" said Boyle. "She's been nominated for a Daytime Emmy at least twelve times." He stuck out his hand. "Detective Art Boyle, Ms. Sargent. Don't mind my partner; she's kind of a cultural snob."

"Can we get ice cream after the movie? Ida's mommy is taking her—"

"Don't interrupt, Ezra." Jenna glared at me. "Why the hell did you call the police?"

"Ummm . . ."

"This doesn't have anything to do with you." Patton stared at her for a few seconds before adding, rather pointedly, "Ma'am."

Boyle stepped in front of his partner. "My wife would kill me if I didn't get an autograph." He threw a crayon and construction paper at the actress.

"Mom, can I—"

"Don't interrupt, Ezra."

"You can make it out to Roselle."

Jenna aimed her chlorine-colored eyes at me. "Was Nate here today?"

"Nate? No. I mean, he left that note, but I wasn't here when he—"

"He's faithful now, you know," she said. "He's getting help."

"I'm glad to hear it," I said.

"Are you? Are you really?"

"Well, to be totally honest, I don't give a rat's . . ." *Stop it, stop it. . . .* I cleared my throat. "I'll tell you what I *do* care about, though—Ezra is such a talented boy, and he did some wonderful artwork today!"

"I drew a taxi, Mommy!"

"That's nice, honey."

As she signed the construction paper for Boyle, I went to Ezra's cubbyhole and grabbed the stack of drawings I'd put inside—colorful sketches of street signs, trees, a bright yellow taxicab with black squares racing up the side.

"Thanks, Ms. Sargent," said Boyle. "Listen, I've got to know something. Why did Blythe try to kill her own brother?"

She delivered her answer directly to me, reading my face like a teleprompter. "He isn't really my brother."

"I knew it! Blythe's father, Marco, stole Lucas when he was a baby, right? Right?"

I held out the stack of artwork, and she took it. "We're in love," she said. "We're going to get married."

"That's terrific."

Boyle said, "No, it isn't; it's disgusting. You were raised as brother and sister."

Finally, Jenna looked at the drawings. I watched her face soften into a smile as she looked at the yellow taxicab.

"I'd say he deserves an IMAX movie and an ice-cream cone, wouldn't you?" I said.

"Yay!"

"Just one scoop, honey." Just as she was about to leave, Jenna shot another glance at my trash can. Then she eyed me up and down, like something she'd ordered out of a catalog and was considering sending back. "I thought you'd be taller," she said.

After Jenna Sargent left, Patton stood staring at the door she'd closed behind her. "What a bitch."

"What do you want?" said Boyle. "She's an actress *and* a Leo. Her kid's lucky she remembers his name."

Boyle pocketed Jenna's signature, then walked over to the window and opened the blinds. "That's the place, right? Next to the Gap?"

"Yeah."

"Well, interestingly enough," said Patton, "nobody lives there."

I looked at her.

"That's not completely accurate," Boyle said. "There is a resident. An old guy by the name of Arnold—not sure whether that's his first or last name. But he's been in the hospital for the past month hooked up to machines."

"The super wasn't aware of anyone watching the place for him," Patton said. "You sure you saw binoculars? I can't imagine anybody wanting to be in that dust trap for more than a minute."

"The super took you inside?"

"Yes, unfortunately."

"Did you get his name and number?"

"*Her*," said Boyle. He handed me an orange Post-it, the name Katia Stavros written in the careful, angular script of an older woman. There was a phone number underneath. "Can I have this?" I asked.

"Sure."

I put it in my desk.

Maybe it was a onetime thing with the binoculars. A squatter who liked breathing dust and looking very closely at a preschool classroom's venetian blinds. I remembered the feeling I'd had yesterday, standing at the pay phone.

"He's watching you. Always."

Okay. A two-time thing. Three, tops.

"I don't know if Krull told you guys," I said, "but this weird guy in Starbucks—"

"The bomb scare?" said Boyle.

Patton shook her head. "Pierce is such a freak."

"I called the guy."

"Why?" Boyle asked.

"He gave me another note," I said. "It's on the desk."

As Boyle picked up the note and started to unfold it, I told Patton, "On the phone he said, 'He's watching you. Always.'"

"Really?"

"He's probably full of shit, this guy. And I feel bad to be wasting your time with it. I know you've had a busy day, with the press conference and—"

"What press conference?" said Patton.

I swallowed hard. "John . . . told me that . . ."

"John should have a press conference so we can find out where the fuck he is. He was questioning Marla's fiancé, but he should have come back, like, hours ago."

"I'm sorry; I hate to interrupt," Boyle said. "But did I hear you say you called him after getting this note?"

"Yeah . . ."

"Because there's no phone number on this."

"Yes, there is, on the bottom, and what do you mean there was no press conf—"

"I'm sorry, Sam," Boyle said slowly, "but I'd like you to take a look at this note, please."

Boyle gave me the piece of paper. Patton might have said something as I read it, but I couldn't hear her—not with the blood pounding in my ears.

He was right. There was no phone number on this note. Just two sentences, written in a shakier hand than the others.

HE KILLED MARLA S. DON'T GET HIM ANGRY AGAIN.

6

Marlamania

Whoever this guy was, he had ample time to put the new note in my bag, because I hardly ever looked inside this black canvas junk receptacle. "Sam's bag," Yale had once announced in his horror-movie voice after spending twenty minutes looking for a breath mint. "Items go in . . . but they *never come out.*"

The fact that I'd found the Marla S. note amid all the debris I carted around was something of a miracle. I remembered what the man had said when I called him: "You found my note." Not *read. Found.*

But when had he planted it? After I talked it over with Boyle and Patton, I decided the most likely scenario was that he'd followed me to the

Gap the previous day and seized the opportunity when I left my purse in the dressing room.

Had he been watching as I called my mother from the pay phone outside? Had he been waiting for me to search for a quarter in the depths of my bag? Had he been angry—angry as Marla's murderer—when I'd used my memorized card number instead? *You found my note.*

"Do you . . . Do you guys really think someone killed Marla because I made him angry?" I asked Krull's partners.

Patton looked straight into my eyes, and I had to brace myself for her answer. The detective was not someone who could look at you and lie—not even about a surprise party, or her opinion of your terrible new haircut. "Marla Soble was murdered because she upset a lunatic," she said. "Not because you did."

I exhaled heavily.

Boyle said, "She's not just trying to make you feel better. She means it."

"I know," I said. "Thank you . . . for meaning it."

"I do want to question the asshole who gave you that note," said Boyle over lunch—which turned out to be chili dogs from a stand on the northwest corner of Washington Square Park. "I want to teach him a lesson about fucking up investigations."

Patton nodded. "That note is just like the billions of false leads we've been getting. You have a high-profile case like this and freaks just pop out of the woodwork. Either they confess to the crime themselves, or they turn in their ex-boyfriend or their landlord or their fuckin' cat. Only difference with this guy is, he contacted you rather than us."

"You think he's one of those Marlamaniacs, who happens to remember Sam's case, too?" Boyle said.

"No way. He was interested in Sam first. Remember she got the 'danger' note before Marla was even identified. He's stalking Sam, trying to scare her into needing him."

"That's exactly what Yale said."

She turned to me. "Soon as we determine his identity, you'll file a restraining order." It was more of a command than a suggestion.

"What's a Marlamaniac?" I asked.

"That's what we're calling her fans," Patton said. "There's this whole convention of them parked outside her building. You should see it. I swear, it's like a zombie movie out there."

I looked at her. "Why would somebody . . ."

"She's pretty and she's dead, I guess. That's all some people need to build a day's activity around."

"Some of 'em asked *me* for my autograph," Boyle said. "Can you imagine?"

"They mighta just thought you were Nick Nolte." Patton winked. "Art's wife thinks he looks like Nick Nolte."

I finished my chili dog and threw my napkin into a nearby trash can.

It felt strange having a conversation like this just twenty or thirty feet away from the crime scene. I'd avoided the area on my way to Sunny Side, but now I couldn't stop looking at the stretch of yellow police tape bordering the easternmost part of the park's giant, shallow fountain, which had since been drained. It was guarded by three uniformed cops—I could see the backs of their heads from where we were standing—but it seemed almost a waste of manpower, considering how many officers strolled through the park on a regular basis.

All those cops walking around a concrete square with practically no trees and a big French arch at one end, dozens and dozens of tourists and NYU students . . . *Weird place to dispose of a corpse.*

"Body was wrapped in garbage bags and packed against the inner side of the fountain with gaffer's tape," said Boyle, who must've seen me staring. "No one noticed until her legs came undone and kind of . . . floated out a little."

"That's a lot of effort."

"In the pouring rain, no less," said Patton. "I still can't figure out why he moved the body. It's not like he was trying to dispose of evidence. How long did he think it would take before someone noticed a body in the Washington Square Park fountain?"

"He wanted her to be found here," Boyle said. "He's physically strong, smart, very fast on his feet, he knows this area like the back of his hand—and he wants the whole world to see that. He's proud of what he did."

"Nice profiling, Art," Patton said.

I looked at them. "Any idea who he might be?"

Patton said quietly, "An NYU professor would know this area like the back of his hand."

"No fucking way," said Boyle. "Did you see the way Valdez is built? My twelve-year-old daughter has bigger muscles. Plus, he's a Cancer. A Cancer would never do something like this. We're talking a Leo on a very bad day, or maybe an Aries with Scorpio rising."

"Valdez certainly had a motive," Patton said. "And he could have had help, could've even contracted someone."

Boyle said, "Yeah, well, hit men are usually more efficient. This was overkill."

"If you don't mind my asking . . . what exactly was done to Marla?" I said.

Boyle finished his third chili dog, then checked

his watch. "Stabbed through the heart," he said. "Thirteen times."

Patton shrugged her shoulders. "Maybe somebody's superstitious."

Boyle headed back to the precinct house, while Patton walked me to the Space. "Why would Krull lie to me about a press conference?" I almost said. But I didn't. To me, the topic was nearly more disturbing than the notes, the binoculars, anything, because I knew the answer: He had somewhere else to go.

"Amanda," I said, as we stopped at a crosswalk. "Did you . . . Have you ever thought your husband might be cheating on you?"

She narrowed her eyes. "Is there something you want to tell me?"

"No, I . . ."

"I'm kidding. But I know why you asked me that."

I swallowed hard. "You do?"

"Sure," she said. "Marla's journal. It's got us all asking ourselves that type of question."

"Oh . . . yeah, of course."

"And it's usually the men who cheat, right?"

I stared at the sidewalk. "It's hardwired into their DNA."

"We're lucky, though, you and I. We got ourselves two of the good guys."

Behind my back, I crossed the fingers on both hands, then my wrists to make it an odd number. "I hope . . ." I started to say, but before I could get out the sentence, I felt it again, the deep shiver of eyes on me. I whirled around fast, but the only person standing behind me was an elderly woman fearfully clutching her pocketbook.

"What's wrong?" Patton said.

"Do you feel like . . . like someone's watching us?"

She turned around. "Just those jackasses." She gestured at three construction workers leaning against some scaffolding on the corner. "Gimme some sugar, baby," said one of them, grabbing his crotch.

I sighed. "Man, I'm getting paranoid."

"Having a stalker will do that to ya." She flipped off the construction workers. "Don't worry; we'll find this guy. We'll get a sketch made up, get the beat cops on it, too."

"You need me to come to the station and give a description?"

"No, Krull saw the dude, too, right?"

"Yeah, and Pierce."

She grinned. "Right. I'm sure he already gave a description to the bomb squad."

I arrived at the box office on time, but was greeted by a sight that made me consider turning around and never coming back. The ticket line stretched all the way to the end of the block—nothing new, but when I got closer I noticed a second line, nearly as long, threading malignantly off the front of the main one.

"Could you please sell me four tickets for next May?" a voice shouted at me.

I hurried past the lines and toward the box office without looking at or speaking to anyone. I had this irrational fear that, if I did, the awful thing might sprout more extensions—like some sort of Hydra with terrible taste in theater.

In the small courtyard, En was involved in his daily therapeutic yoga pose, balancing on the palms of his hands, a leg wrapped around each taut elbow. He looked like something out of Cirque du Soleil—but Shell seemed far more interested in the latest issue of *Marie Claire.*

I said, "What do you call that pose, En?"

"The Frog." He cast a glance at Shell. "It helps release *stored sexual tension.*"

"Sorry I asked."

Before I went into the box office, I said to Shell, "Any idea what's going on with the line out there?"

"You mean *our* line, or Tabitha's?"

I hurried into the subscription room, where Roland was adding up a pile of credit-card receipts, into the box office, past Yale, who was looking at his *Mikado* sheet music.

We still had ten minutes before we were officially open, but I made for the ticket window anyway and pushed aside the shade.

"Don't do that," said Yale. "They attack when they see movement."

I stared through the window. "Shell's right."

Yale glanced over my shoulder. "Yep. A star is born."

Tabitha was standing in her usual spot, at the front of the ticket line. She wore a sleeveless black cocktail dress from the fifties—the most skin I'd ever seen her show. And she was signing autographs.

At least twenty people were waiting in line to meet someone who'd suddenly become famous for waiting in line. "Now that's just insane."

Yale said nothing—he just reached into his jeans pocket, pulled out a rolled-up *Shakespearean Idol* program and tossed it to me.

On the second page was a bubbly signature, wrought in hot-pink ink: *'Til Death, Tabitha Meeks!*

"You're not going to set her house on fire, are you?"

"Very funny."

"You know, until about an hour ago, I would have thought you're the most pathetic person on earth for getting that signature."

"What changed your mind?"

"Marlamaniacs."

"You mean—"

"John's partners told me about them. Fans of a dead woman, can you imagine? They ask cops for their autographs."

"So that's who they were," said Yale.

"You saw them?"

"On my way to work. I *thought* they looked too weird to be protestors."

Yale unlocked the ticket drawer. And, for a long moment, he just stared at the lined-up cardboard strips, as if they were tea leaves and could tell him the future.

"What's wrong?" I asked.

"I just . . ." He took a deep breath. "I'm glad you don't live there anymore."

"Me too."

"I mean, she was a woman with dark, straight hair like yours. And she was your age, living in the place where you'd be living—"

"You're saying it could've been me."

He nodded. "If you never met John. He probably saved your life when you think about it—and not for the first time either."

"You sound like quite the fan yourself."

"Everybody loves an action hero."

That's what I'm afraid of. "He didn't call for me, did he?"

"No. Was he supposed to? Oh, my God, is he okay?"

"He's fine, Yale. Everybody's perfectly fine."

"I'm being melodramatic, aren't I?"

"Yeah, a little."

"I'll be glad when this damn *Mikado* audition is over so I can stop obsessing over the idea of random executions. Last night, I dreamed I had to cut Peter's head off with a letter opener."

I rolled my eyes at him. "It's Gilbert and Sullivan."

"But it's dark. It's very dark and . . . complex."

"I think you're getting into the role too deep. I think you're rehearsing too much. They call it light opera for a reason."

"I'm trying out for the role of a hired killer."

"A hired killer named *KoKo!*"

Before Yale could reply, Roland strode into the ticketing room, shouting, "Okay, people! Places!" and threw the shades open.

Just like always, Tabitha said, "Hello," so quietly I could barely read the word on her lips, and placed forty dollars through the metal slot under my window. I handed her the front-row-center ticket I always pulled for her, said into the microphone, "Enjoy the show, Tabitha."

"Tabs."

"Excuse me?"

"I'm trying out a new nickname, okay, Sam?"

"Oh. Sure . . . Tabs."

She winked a glittery, kohl-smudged eye at me. "Thanks, honeychild."

As Tabitha moved away from the window, followed by her small entourage of autograph seekers, I turned to Yale. "A star is definitely born."

"Tabs is not good, though. What she should do is drop the last name and just be Tabitha, with an exclamation point . . . like Evita! or Liza with a Z!"

"What about Tabby?"

"Only if she were a famous *Cats* fan."

I winced.

As I ran the credit card of the next man in line, Yale said, "You know what? You're right. Yesterday, I told you not to overreact to your obsessed fan, and here I am overreacting to light opera. At least the fan is real."

"Oh, he's real, all right."

"What?"

"Nothing. Get your audition over with and we'll talk."

When break time finally came, I borrowed Yale's cell and tried both Krull and my mother, but got only their voice mails. *Where are you people?*

I poked my head in the theater, where Yale was onstage, singing the last lines of "To Sit in Solemn Silence" for Tabitha and six of her followers.

"That was wonderful," Tabitha called out as the rest of the small group applauded. "But could you try and make it, like . . . twenty percent sexier?"

I put Yale's phone on top of his stack of sheet music and crept out.

In the courtyard, En and Shell were sitting on a checkered picnic blanket, eating slices of what appeared to be purple meat. "Red-wine chicken!" Shell called out. "Want some?"

"No, thanks."

I'd worked up a decent appetite, and was planning on trying a new diner at the end of the block. But the closer I got to it, the more reluctant I was to go in. It wasn't so much the sight of Shell's Concord-grape chicken that did it, but a vague sense of foreboding no doubt brought on by the binoculars and the new note. I couldn't imagine sitting down in an unfamiliar place with strangers all around me.

Don't get him angry again.

There was a Subway sandwich shop across the street, where I'd picked up lunch plenty of times. But that didn't appeal either. So I turned right on Seventh and walked five blocks uptown, to Twenty-sixth Street. What I really wanted, I knew now, was to see the Marlamaniacs.

The first thing I noticed was the shrine they'd made for her: A four-foot-tall oval of pink and white carnations with a gilt-framed newspaper photo of Marla and Lucky at the center, it was propped up next to the front door. At the top was a white banner, with black, cursive letters that leaped out at you: *A new angel in heaven.*

I didn't see the Marlamaniacs at first because they were sitting. But when I got a little closer, there they were—at least fifteen of them, on the sidewalk, on blankets and lawn chairs, eating bag lunches while listening to news stations on portable radios. If you didn't know any better, you'd think they were waiting in line for *Star Wars* tickets.

A year and a half ago, when I used to live here, my downstairs neighbor had knocked on my door and found a serial killer on the other side. She'd actually been the first person murdered in there, and in a very unpleasant way, but as far as I could remember, it had never earned her a fan club.

I looked at them—more women than men, all white in the worst sense of the word—pasty and lusterless, like they'd spent their whole lives underground.

As I got closer to the door, one of the women jumped to her feet and stepped in front of me. "Did you know her?" she asked.

Her face was so wan and beige you could instantly forget it, even while looking at her.

"No," I said. "Did you?"

I walked up to the shrine. After 9/11, I'd seen plenty of shrines around the city. Always, they gave me a lump in my throat because the items placed on them were so deeply personal—Saint Christopher's medals and family snapshots, company softball jerseys and dried prom corsages, postcards that said, *I love you and miss you,* in ink that still looked wet.

This one was different. I knew the Marlamaniacs had made it because it was so tidy, so generic. It contained no evidence of a life. Maybe Marla Soble especially liked pink and white carnations, but I doubted it. "She's pretty and she's dead," Patton had said. And for this group, that was more than enough. She was their new angel in heaven.

I thought of asking which one of them had made the shrine when I noticed something about it that I hadn't seen before.

Resting against the bottom of the carnation oval was a single Sterling rose, its stem bent in two. "Whoa."

"Murderer!" screamed the woman I'd encountered at the door. For a second, I thought she was talking to me, but then all the Marlamaniacs joined in, rising to their feet, hissing and booing.

I whirled around and saw, moving through the double doors of my old apartment building, a slight man in wire-rimmed glasses surrounded by cops. Professor Gil Valdez.

A man yelled, "Burn in hell, killer!"

Three uniforms piled into a waiting van, then Marla's fiancé, and then two more. Just before he got in, I caught a glimpse of his face—and saw a depth of pain that was beyond tears.

Someone he loved is dead.

Another group left the building—obviously plainclothes detectives. I didn't see Krull, but I did spot Pierce and his two partners. "Zachary!" I called out.

"Hey, Sam! Stopping by the old homestead?" Pierce told his partners he'd catch up with them, then signed a few autographs before sauntering up to me. "Wacky group, huh? I feel like Mick Jagger or something."

"Have you seen John?" I asked.

"Not lately. I've been at this crime scene for a while, though."

I watched his face. "I wanted to find out how the press conference went."

"Oh, that," he said. "It never happened."

"You mean it was supposed to?"

"Well, yeah. But the commissioner canceled it because I guess he realized we have nothing to say."

I exhaled heavily. "Oh, I can't tell you how happy that makes me."

"That we have nothing to say?"

"No. See, Patton knew nothing about the press conference, so I thought—"

"No offense to her, but she's a new mom," Pierce said. "Her memory's like grated cheese 'cause her kid's such a crappy sleeper."

An explanation. A normal, reasonable explanation from the man who thinks terrorists are targeting branches of Starbucks and a firefighter's ghost haunts his apartment. I kissed Pierce on the cheek. "Thank you."

"Hey." He grinned. "We should cancel press conferences more often."

I glanced down at the bent Sterling rose. *There's an explanation for that, too. Maybe Marla happened to like them. Or maybe one of her fans does.*

"So," said Pierce. "You wanna take a look at your old apartment?" And it hit me that I did, very much.

When the elevator doors opened, and Pierce and I stepped out onto the twelfth floor, I was struck first by the complete lack of noise. Not a sound in the stairwell, no music or conversation from behind the thin apartment doors. No cooking smells, either, which was even stranger. Thinking about it now, I could hardly recall a time, traveling between the elevator and my apartment, when I hadn't smelled bacon or frying onions.

Did anyone live on this floor anymore? Was everyone dead?

I coughed. It seemed to echo. And as we walked toward my old apartment, I could almost hear each individual rug fiber pressing against the soles of my shoes and springing back.

How I hated this type of quiet, the kind that closes in on you like fog, the kind that shrieks in your ears.

I had to say something to Pierce, just to make it go away. "So . . ."

"No, it's not haunted," he said. "I know what a ghost feels like, and there aren't any spirits in your old place."

"Okay. Well . . . that's nice to know."

As we got closer to the apartment, I saw what looked like a typewritten note stuck to the door. For half a second, I thought, *A fan letter to Marla.*

But then I realized it was just the police seal, freshly broken by Pierce and his crew.

I remembered Professor Valdez's face.

As the detective produced a set of keys from his pocket, I said, "He didn't do it, you know."

I watched Pierce calmly open the five dead bolts, as if he had always lived here. "Who, Valdez?" he said as he undid the last one. "I think you'd feel different if you saw her journal."

Before he opened the door, he said, "It's pretty stuffy, I'm warning you. We were only in here for a very short time—the rest of it was checking out stairwells, talking to the super, some of the neighbors, so . . ."

"I can handle stuffy."

I followed him inside, and what hit me first was a strong smell of citrus and soap, probably Marla's shampoo.

How strange that a smell could outlive a person. The apartment had an air conditioner in the window, I knew. But that was turned off and the window was closed, so that lemony scent hung in the dark, still air like a solid, breathing thing. As if she were standing there, watching.

"Was Professor Valdez in here?" I asked.

"Yep."

"He cried, didn't he?"

"People cry for all sorts of reasons."

Pierce turned on a light, and I was glad for how normal the place looked, save the pale coating of fingerprint dust on the small coffee table, the kitchen counter, the small, French provincial desk where Marla had probably kept her computer before the police took it for clues.

No blood spatter. No chalk outline. Of course not; her body was found in the park. *Why did he move her?*

"Hey, Sam, were your floors always that crappy? Because I was thinking he might have used some kind of corrosive soap to clean up her blood."

"They were always that crappy." Slowly, I walked around the room. She had a pullout couch against the same wall where I'd put mine. It was the same shape as mine too, only instead of beige velour, hers was white, with pink ribbon stripes running down it. Unlike my furniture, all of which I'd bought in two hours from a place called Rent 2 Own, Marla's looked as if she'd put some thought into it. There was an actual color scheme. She had real candles in her candlesticks, vases that didn't look like they came with the flowers. I spotted a drooping bouquet at the center of her coffee table that was probably stunning a week ago. A dozen roses of every color, four of them Sterlings. *See, she did like them.* "I bet Professor Valdez gave her those."

"Maybe."

She'd arranged everything more or less the same as I had; in a space that small, you don't have much choice. Marla had put her dinette set near the window, too—hers was distressed white wood, with high-backed chairs. I noticed a black stripe across one of them, and realized, only then, that it was the strap of my bag. I'd hung it on the dinette chair, just as I'd always done when I got home from work.

"I never saw this place when you lived here. I bet it looked awesome." Pierce was standing in front of a large white bookshelf. It covered the entire wall where I'd hung *Reverie,* and was packed tight with books, bright and faded, paperback and hardcover—bought for reading, not decoration, because the colors didn't mesh at all. The detective faced it, hands clasped behind his back, as if admiring a museum piece. "See? She alphabetized her books," he said.

But I didn't respond. I was staring at the exposed brick wall.

The heart looked bigger in person than it had in the paper, and had dried rusty brown. As I looked at it, it was easy to pretend it wasn't blood at all, especially considering the way the killer had applied it. In the black-and-white newspaper picture, the line forming the heart had looked smooth and even, like it had been drawn with a paintbrush or, more likely, the victim's bloody clothing. But looking at it now, some areas were much darker than others, and the drips were more obvious. On parts of the line, I discerned four thick grooves, which, as a preschool teacher, I recognized instantly. Finger paint.

He had drawn the heart with his hands.

"Sam," said Pierce.

I turned and saw him standing behind me, paging through one of Marla's books.

"Check it out," he said, holding it up so I could see the cover. *The Art of Caring.* "It's signed!"

Suddenly the door swung open so hard that the

brass knob cracked the wall. I was dimly aware of my mother's best-selling book falling out of Pierce's hand, as we both spun around staring like trapped, doomed rats.

In the doorway stood Krull. His hard black gaze shot from my face to Pierce's and back again. Even from across the room, I could smell cigarettes. "What are you doing here?" he said.

"Jesus," said Pierce. "You scared the shit out of me, dude."

Krull glared at me. "Sam, have you been taking night classes at the police academy?"

"Uhhh . . . no. Hey, where were you all day?"

"Because last time I checked, this was a fucking crime scene, and you were a civilian unrelated to this case!"

Pierce said, "Whoa, man. Take a chill pill."

"You take a chill pill, you little prick."

I was aware of my stomach contracting, of my hands, balled into fists, the muscles in my calves and thighs clenching up until my whole body was tight, like a rubber band. I spoke through my teeth. "You didn't answer my question," I said.

Krull glowered at Pierce, and all I could think of was a rattlesnake, ready to devour a mouse. "I am sick and tired of you—especially the crush you have on my girlfriend," he said. "It gets in the way of your work. And it makes you a crappy cop."

For a long time, no one moved, and it felt to me like we were trapped there forever: Krull, Pierce, Marla and me. All of us frozen, angry ghosts.

Until finally, Pierce said, "Go fuck yourself, John." And walked out of the apartment.

From the end of the hallway, I heard the ping of the elevator, the doors opening and closing.

"What is wrong with you?" I said.

His gaze was fixed on the bloody heart. "You shouldn't be here."

"Yeah, well, I was just leaving."

Just before I got to the door, I turned around. "I had no idea you could be so mean," I said.

But Krull didn't reply. He just kept staring at that smeared, rust-brown valentine, as if I didn't exist.

7

Ready to Listen

When I finally got back to the box office, I was half an hour late and Roland's mouth was a thin scratch of frustration.

"I'm so sorry; I—"

"No excuses. You're working the phones, and you get no breaks, even for the bathroom."

"I'm—"

"No excuses."

At least Yale was working the other phone. If Shell were to so much as smile at me—let alone offer me a baked good right now—I couldn't be held responsible for my actions.

"What happened to you?" said Yale. "You look like you've seen a ghost."

"That's a good way of putting it."

"Where did you—"

"I don't want to talk, Yale; I just *don't.*"

Fortunately, the phone orders rolled in one on top of the next, leaving no opportunity to talk even if I'd wanted to. There was something so comfortably dispassionate about taking down credit-card numbers and expiration dates. I could have done it a lot later than six thirty p.m., when The Space's phones officially closed.

Yale and I alphabetized our receipts and handed them to Roland, just as En and Shell were opening up the will-call window for the final stretch of their evening.

"Nice job, all of you," said Roland. "Even Samantha."

"Thanks."

He patted me on the shoulder. "Don't let it happen again."

"Yeah, really," said En. "We had dinner reservations, but we had to cancel them because you two got switched to the phones." He looked at Roland. "Come to think of it, that's not entirely fair."

"I'll buy you guys dinner."

"Deal."

As Yale and I stepped out into the courtyard, I remembered Krull as I'd last seen him, the coldness in his eyes as he stared up at that brick wall. I couldn't believe he hadn't called to apologize, couldn't believe he'd just let me go.

"You feel like telling me what happened?" Yale said.

"Oh, nothing . . . I stopped by my old place to see the Marlamaniacs, and I wound up having a little . . . spat with Krull."

"Well, you should get home right now and talk things out. Remember, it's the differences between us that make us realize we're not alone."

"Who said that? It sounds familiar."

"Sydney Stark-Leiffer."

I smiled. "Want to get a drink or something?"

"Can't," he said. "Going straight home to bed. I'm rehearsing at dawn tomorrow."

"I really hope you get this part."

Yale gave me a quick hug good-night, then headed uptown to his happy home.

Guess it's time to go back to Stuy Town and talk things out. I started to leave the courtyard—but I was stopped by the sound of Shell shrieking my name into the box office microphone.

When I jogged back to the front of the will-call line, Shell reached under the counter and produced a triangular note. "I almost forgot—some guy left this for you," she said, and slipped it through the metal slot.

Throw it away; don't let me have it, I wanted to say. But I couldn't keep myself from taking the note, from opening it and reading.

"He sort of looked like a terrorist," said Shell.

En said, "That's racist, honey."

"No, it isn't. He's not black."

The note said, HE'S ANGRY. And then, at the bottom of the paper, in letters so small the words were barely visible: WATCH YOUR BACK.

Anger coursed up my spine, through the tangle of my nervous system. "Fucking asshole." I ripped the note into tiny little pieces, then threw them up in the air like confetti. "I hope you're watching now, loser!" I shouted. *"Leave me alone!"*

My voice bounced off the pavement. I noticed heads turning away in the ticket takers' line, the way heads always turn away from the insane. Then I heard En's voice through the microphone. "Whoa, Sam. How do you *really* feel about this guy?"

Nervous laughter from the theatergoers, studded with barely whispered comments: "Only in New York, right?"

"... oughta think about antianxiety meds ..."

"... that time of the month."

I ignored all of it.

I ran down to the sidewalk and stuck my arm out. Like something out of a dream, a cab pulled up fast, but I didn't get in right away. I couldn't move. The driver rolled down his window. "Don't you want a taxi, lady?" he said. But still, I was immobile—a statue on the pavement.

"Something wrong?" he said.

Oh, how there was. There was something breathtakingly wrong with this cab. It was the ad on top: My mother's face, huge and smiling. And under it, the words, DR. SYDNEY STARK-LEIFFER. SHE'S IN NEW YORK CITY, AND SHE'S READY TO LISTEN!

"We apologize for the delay, but please stay on the line. Sydney cares about you."

"Bullshit," I said to the recorded voice. Not that I was counting, but we'd had this exact exchange, that voice and I, at least ten times in the past half hour alone.

Bullshit, Sydney cares about me.

I'd been trying to reach my mother at WLUV (*Who do you have to bribe to get call letters like that?*) ever since I'd learned, from the exhausted-sounding switchboard operator, that yes, *the* Sydney Stark-Leiffer was counseling callers live from WLUV's studios in Midtown Manhattan. Just like the ad on top of the cab said. And she'd been doing so for the past *two weeks*.

What kind of a mother doesn't consult with her daughter before moving cross-country to her city? What kind of mother never even tells her daughter after she gets there? What kind of mother does that two whole weeks ago?!

"We apologize for the—"

"Bullshit!" Jake jumped out of my lap. I threw the

cordless receiver across the room, heard plastic hitting the hard floor, a small piece—probably the battery cover—skittering across the room.

"Bullshitbullshitbullshitbullshit!" I was screaming like our neighbors did every night—so loud the walls seemed to vibrate, and I didn't even hear the door opening.

I doubled over, scrunching my face up to keep from crying because I would not let Sydney Stark-Leiffer make me cry on top of everything else, and that's when I felt Krull's arms around me. "Hey, hey, hey," he said.

I leaned into his chest, felt the cool cloth of his short-sleeved shirt, inhaled the clean, plain smell of the soap he used, the leather of his shoulder holster, and thought, *Thank you.*

"What's wrong, Sam?" he said again.

And all I could say was, "My mother."

For a few moments, I was back in seventh grade again, in the parking lot at sunset, waiting for her. My throat clenched up, and I felt that maddening heat pressing into the backs of my eyeballs. *Don't cry.*

"She is moving here after all?" Krull said.

"Moved. She moved. She's here, and she never even . . ."

Krull sighed, rubbing my back. "Some people don't think," he said. "Some people do things, and they're so wrapped up in . . . doing those

things that they don't think about how those . . .
things . . . might hurt other people."

I pulled away from him, looking into his eyes.
"Stop saying *things*."

He kissed me gently. "I'm sorry," he said. "I'm
sorry your mother moved to New York without
telling you, and I'm sorry I was such a dickhead
this afternoon. You don't deserve either one of
us."

"What about poor Pierce?" I said. "He got the
brunt of your dickheadedness."

"I couldn't get hold of him, but I left a case of
beer outside his apartment. Hopefully, he'll get
home before his neighbors steal it."

"Or his ghost."

"Yeah, his ghost . . . I'm so sorry, Sam."

"It's okay."

For a long while, we sat on the floor, just looking at each other. I realized we hadn't looked at
each other in a long time; not like this, anyway.
When did we start making love with our eyes closed?

"You know what?" I said. "On top of everything else, I can't even get her on the phone. Her
stupid radio station has had me on hold for the
last decade."

Krull glanced at the crumpled receiver on the
floor. "Can't get anybody on the phone now," he
said.

"Oh, shit, I broke the phone."

"It's fixable." He cupped my face in his hand, and I realized it had been a long time since he'd done this, too—touched my face.

"Everything's fixable," Krull said. "Isn't it?"

He asked what I felt like for dinner, and I said, "I feel like Indian." So we decided to have dinner at one of the Indian restaurants on Sixth and Second—the first time we'd gone out to eat in more than two months. Krull locked his gun in the safe, then changed out of his work clothes and into jeans and the vintage black Iron Maiden T-shirt I'd bought him for his last birthday. (*"If you can't beat a heavy-metal obsession,"* I'd explained, *"at least make it look good."* And it did. I loved that shirt on him to the point of envying it.)

The night was cooler and clearer than it had been in weeks. You'd almost expect to see stars in the purple sky. And as we walked to Sixth Street, holding hands, I was aware that the humid air had an autumnal undercurrent—that sneaking crispness that made you know, within weeks, leaves would be dying.

We didn't say much on the way there, but it wasn't an uncomfortable silence. In fact, what I noticed most of all (other than two buses with Sydney's face on the side) was how comfortable I *did* feel, for a change. Like I wasn't being watched.

I wondered if Boyle and Patton had told Krull that someone had been examining my classroom through binoculars, or that I'd received three additional notes from a man now deemed a stalker . . . but not enough to bring any of it up just yet. Instead I said, "Fall's coming. Can you smell it?"

"You said that last year."

"I did?"

"The morning of September eleventh. I was leaving for work, and that's exactly what you said."

"Oh . . . I . . . I didn't remember."

He gave my hand a squeeze. "Seems like a long time ago, huh?"

When we got to the row of Indian restaurants, Krull said, "Pick one," and I pointed at the place with the friendliest-looking host at the door.

When we got closer, the host called us "happy newlyweds," and instead of correcting him, we both just smiled.

We ordered a bottle of wine and two different kinds of nan to start. When we were nearly through with both, I said in my best cheesy-TV-cop voice, "So, Five-O, I'm sure you heard about Monsieur Perp's letter-writing campaign."

Krull smiled. "Who?"

"You know . . . the weird little guy with the accent."

"The Starbucks guy?"

"Yeah, he's sent me three more notes since then."

"You're kidding me."

"Patton and Boyle know about it. I tried to call you first, but you were—"

"What did they say?"

"Patton and Boyle?"

"The notes."

"Oh . . . just . . . They were about some name-less person being angry. *He.* When I talked to him on the phone, he said—"

"You talked to him on the phone?"

"Yeah. He said this person, whose name he doesn't know, is always watching me. And planning something."

"Jesus, Sam. I was going to run a reverse on him, but I . . . forgot. I'll do it tonight, from our computer."

"Don't worry about it," I said. "He's just a fan."

"A fan?"

"That's what Boyle and Patton think. Yale too. As soon as they determine his identity, I'll file a restraining order. That'll show him."

"I . . . I haven't been there for you, have I?"

I polished off the rest of my wine, listening to the words slur as they came out of my mouth. "Why would you shay that? Listen to me, I shound like Carol Channing."

"I'm the one who should be protecting you from him. Not those guys."

"You want to hear shome—something—funny?" I said.

"Yeah?"

"He sends me this note, right? Leaves it in my purse—I can't believe I actually found it in there."

"How did he get to your purse?"

"At the Gap, I think."

"Where you bought that new shirt—"

"Anyway, all these notes are about some mysterious *he* or *him* or whatever. . . ."

Krull nodded.

"Well, this one says, 'He killed Marla S. Don't get him angry again.' And I'm racking my brain, 'Who did I piss off the night Marla was killed?' And the only person I can figure out—the only *him* I got angry that night—was *you!*"

Krull stared at me.

"I can't believe I just said that."

"You think I—"

"I don't think anything, John. Obviously it's the wine."

"But you said—"

"The point I was trying to make . . . before my tongue got tied in knots . . . was that this guy's full of shit. He wants me to get all scared and paranoid of every other 'he' I know, so I go running to him for help. It could have been Yale or

Roland or your father or Jake I pissed off that night—wouldn't make any difference to him because he has no idea."

His eyes cut into mine. "Oh."

"So there's no point in running a reverse." I cleared my throat.

Krull called the waiter over, ordered lamb saag, chicken vindaloo and a pitcher of water. And as he scanned the menu for more ideas, I flashed, for a moment, on Ezra, gazing so seriously at *The Runaway Bunny* and his loving, shape-shifting mother. "There's this boy in my class who breaks my heart a little."

"Let me guess," he said. "His dad's not around, and his mom is a huge piece of work."

"How did you know?"

"Because there's always a kid like that in your class, and that kid always breaks your heart."

I stared into his eyes, feeling my own eyes starting to water. "Why do the dads always leave? Make their kids wish they'd never been born? Is selfishness hardwired into male DNA? Is . . . total disloyalty and . . . and weakness?"

Krull said nothing; he just watched me.

"Yikes," I said. "Don't know where that came from."

"I do."

"I didn't mean to be such a downer, John. Can we please start over?"

"Tell me about the rest of your day," he said. And for a while, it was as if we actually had started over. Our conversation jumped easily from one topic to the next: Yale's upcoming *Mikado* audition, Tabitha's newfound celebrity, the chalk city I drew in class, Shell's purple chicken, my decision never to speak to my mother again.

Until finally I said what I'd wanted to say all night. "Where were you today, John? Why couldn't I get hold of you?"

He swallowed the rest of his last glass of wine before speaking again.

Krull had never been that much of a drinker, so, big as he was, alcohol tended to show early on him. "It's . . . I had . . . responsibilities. . . ."

"Oh." I reached out and took his hand. "What do you say we talk about it later? Maybe tomorrow, after we get through with our hangovers."

He gazed at my hand, clasping his. And when he looked up again . . . maybe it was the dim lighting in the restaurant, or perhaps the dependable melodrama of my imagination, but what I saw in his eyes was a sorrow so deep, it stopped my breathing for a few seconds. "Sam," he said. "What would you do if you found out something about me? Something that . . . isn't good?"

Oh, please let it be the cigarettes. Please let him say, "I must confess: I'm a closet smoker." And I'll act surprised and think, "There goes my secret litmus test, but oh, well. At least it's only cigarettes."

I said, "Is it the cigarettes?"

"No, Sam. It's not."

I opened my mouth. But before I could make any more words come out, I felt a hand on my shoulder, heard a voice say, "Am I glad to see you!"

I looked up and there—in the world's worst answer to my prayers—stood Nate Gundersen, staring down at me as if I were his favorite toy from childhood.

He was wearing a plain white T-shirt, pale khaki pants, white sneakers—all of it so light and clean against his tanned skin and shining blond hair that he seemed to glow.

I wondered if this look of Nate's wasn't an attempt to advertise his newfound purity. *He's faithful now. He's getting help.* Was step eight at Whores Anonymous a shopping spree at Banana Republic?

For lack of anything better to say, I introduced him to the man sitting across from me—dark eyed and brooding, a screaming corpse on the front of his black Iron Maiden T-shirt.

"I know who you are," said Krull.

"Really?" I said. "I thought you said you didn't."

"I know. Who he is."

"John Krull. That sounds familiar," Nate said. "You don't act, do you?"

"I don't act." For the first time, I truly understood the expression *If looks could kill.*

"John's a detective," I said.

"Oh, right," Nate said. "You were in all the newspapers two years ago. You're the one from the . . . with Samantha . . ."

"Bingo."

"We have a lot in common."

"Meaning?"

"The character I play just became a police commissioner." Nate had crouched down next to my chair, his arm resting on the back. Considering how perilously close he was to having the shit kicked out of him, the self-confidence of this gesture was staggering.

"I need to talk to you," Nate said to me. "Alone."

I widened my eyes, thinking, *The balls on you.* But that was always what had gotten Nate Gundersen everything he wanted—not his looks or his charm or his Phi Beta Kappa key. Not even his parents, who adored their youngest son so much they'd flown in from Minnesota every time he was in a play at Stanford, staying throughout its entire run, even if he was only in one scene.

It was the balls on him.

"I'm . . . I think I'm kind of busy right now,

Nate?" My voice came out about an octave higher than usual. *What is wrong with me?*

"Please, just for one minute." He looked at Krull. "I promise I'll bring her back in one piece."

"Knock yourself out," said my boyfriend.

I looked at him. "Don't I get a say in this?"

"You've had your say," Krull said quietly. "I heard you, loud and clear."

Once we were outside the restaurant door, and once he had finished autographing a copy of *Soap Opera Digest* that the host had just today purchased from the deli across the street (*"What a happy coincidence! Please make it out to 'My number one fan!' "*), Nate shot a quick look through the window at the back of Krull's head and said, "Sorry I interrupted you like that."

"That's okay," I said. "He was just about to tell me he has three hours to live."

Nate put both hands on my shoulders. I had the sensation of being watched again, and instinctively turned my head up to the apartments over the Indian restaurants, thinking, *Binoculars?* But then I noticed Krull's face, snapping back to profile. I didn't blame him. I'd have been watching, too.

"Samantha," Nate said. "There was a woman killed, and she lived in your old apartment."

"I know that."

He didn't let go. I could feel his grip tightening

on my shoulders, and when I looked up at his face I noticed a sheen to it, a wetness that seeped into the collar of his T-shirt. I tried to remember the last time I'd seen Nate sweat when it had nothing to do with treadmills or stage lights . . . and drew a blank. *What is going on with you? Why are you sweating at nine p.m. on the first cool night in weeks? Why are you in the East Village? Why are you touching me?*

I glared into his eyes. And, at that moment, I saw all that confidence—the balls on him—dissolve into fear. He didn't even look like Nate Gundersen anymore. He looked like someone wearing a pretty mask that was on too tight.

"What's wrong?" I said.

"I knew her."

"Marla Soble?"

"Yes."

I swallowed hard. "What a happy coincidence."

"I met her a week ago. When I went to her apartment. I was looking for you."

"Why?"

"I wanted to apologize. You know . . . step seven."

"How did you get the address?"

"I Googled you. I guess I got an old listing or something, but . . . I went there. And . . . she answered the door. She knew who I was. She'd seen me on TV, and . . . her dog liked me."

"Okay . . ."

"She made me a cup of coffee and we talked about Lucas. How it makes sense that he forgives Blythe for trying to murder him because he knows she's only trying to get back at their with-holding father—the father's the real enemy. I compared Blythe to Medea—loving but vengeful. And then Marla . . . And then we . . ."

"Oh, God, you didn't."

"I went off the wagon."

"You were the one she cheated with?!"

"Not the only one, I'm sure."

"You have to tell the police. You can tell John right now."

"I can't tell the police, Samantha. You don't un-derstand. It will get in the papers. The fans would freak out—I could lose my job. And . . . Jenna. Jenna would fucking kill me."

I stared at him. "But you could help them find the murderer."

"How could I possibly—"

"You can give them information. Like . . . was Marla afraid?"

"Of course not."

"Not of you, for God's sake. Did she tell you anything—maybe her fiancé was mad at her? Or she owed somebody money or—"

"All we talked about was *Live and Let Live*, Samantha. She was a fan. I didn't even know her last name until I saw it in the paper."

"Unbelievable. What am I talking about? Of course it's believable."

"I lost control. . . ." He glanced over at Krull, who was now talking to our waiter. "Don't tell him, please," he said. "It's my life, Samantha. My whole fucking life will be ruined. . . ."

Nate's voice faded away. Maybe he could tell what I was thinking: *Let's talk about ruining other people's lives for just one minute.*

I would have said exactly that. Then I would have walked back into the restaurant, leaving him alone on Second Avenue, burning with guilt over what he'd done to Jenna, what he'd done to me, what he'd done to who knew how many other women, men and transgendered individuals during the fifteen or so years he'd been bringing new meaning to the phrase *sexually active.*

But there was something about Nate's face that stopped me. Was it the sweat? "How did you find me here?" I asked.

"I've been looking for you ever since Veronica and her mother showed up at the studio with the pass I gave you. She told me your address at Stuy Town, and when you weren't in your apartment, I started checking every bar and restaurant on the Lower East Side."

"But why?"

"I needed to tell you."

"Nate, what do I have to do with—"

"Because you should know how lucky you are that you don't love me anymore."

Gently I removed his hands from my shoulders, then held them for a while before letting them drop. "I've known that for years," I said.

I saw a hint of the old brightness coming back into his eyes. "You have to tell the police. They can keep it confidential, but they need to know—if only to rule out any DNA of yours they might find in her apartment."

He winced.

"Sorry, but it's true."

"Okay. I'll make you a deal."

"What . . ."

"Let me tell Jenna tonight first. We were supposed to see *Shakespearean Idol* together, but at least I can meet her at the theater afterward, take her out for coffee or something. In twenty-four hours, I promise I'll tell the police."

I looked at him.

"Please, Samantha, just one day. For Jenna. And Ezra?"

"Oh, okay." I sighed.

He took my hand and shook it.

"Who did you buy your tickets from, anyway?"

"That guy, En."

"You sleep with him too?"

"That's not funny." He thought for a few moments. "Well, maybe it's a little funny."

Before he started off in the direction of the Space, Nate said, "Marla was nice."

"She seemed like she was. I saw the articles—"

"But she wasn't you." He touched the side of my face, his fingertips barely grazing the skin. "She wasn't you."

By the time I got back to the table, Krull was sitting in front of an empty plate. "What did he want?" he asked.

I closed my eyes. *You gave him your word. Just 'til tomorrow.* "He wanted an audition for *Shakespearean Idol*. He thought I might be able to introduce him to the director."

"Ah," he said. "Couldn't get his agent to do that, huh?"

"I . . . guess not."

Krull put his fork down and looked at me. "Listen, I've got to take care of a few things back at the precinct."

"At nine o'clock at night?"

"Stay as long as you want. I already paid the bill."

"John," I said. "I'm sorry, I—"

"You know what? I don't want to know what Nate Gundersen really wanted from you. I don't want to know how he knew enough to look for you at this restaurant, which you picked out. I don't want to know why he was holding on to your shoulders like that. Some . . . pieces of information . . . are better off as secrets." He stood up.

"Wait a minute!" I said, much too loudly.

Other customers turned to look. Ready for drama. Ready to be entertained by two people they'd never met.

But Krull cut it all short—the public show, the comfort of this first cool September night, the rest of what I'd been planning to say. "I have evidence against you," he said. "I didn't believe it before, but now I do."

8

'Til Death

After Krull left, I sat in the restaurant for quite a while, staring at his empty chair and shoving Indian food in my mouth. *What evidence?* I kept thinking.

"Would you like something to read?" said the host.

"No, thanks."

"I must insist," he said. "A young woman alone at dinnertime needs a place to put her eyes."

"Oh, okay."

Carefully, he placed that copy of *Soap Opera Digest* in front of me. "Please be gentle with it," he said, pointing out Nate Gundersen's fresh signature at the bottom of a cigarette ad.

Nate himself was on the cover of the magazine,

which I imagined was a pretty common occurrence. I looked at the picture—shirtless and scowling, his chest glistening with fake sweat.

I read the block letters that ran across the leg of his tight black jeans: L&LL: LUCAS IS ALIVE—AND HE WANTS REVENGE! The print was red—like a Valentine, like wet blood. In his left hand, Nate clasped a large hunting knife that glinted under the studio lights, and didn't look like a prop at all.

I got the host's attention and gave him back the magazine. "Thank you," I said. "But I don't feel like putting my eyes here tonight."

I looked at my watch. Nine thirty. If I took a cab, I could make it in time for the end of *Shakespearean Idol* and get Nate to call Krull personally. Jenna too. She owed me one for showing up at Sunny Side so late and bitchy. And he owed me three years and three thousand miles.

I hurried out the door and grabbed a taxi.

I squeezed into the back of the theater just as Corky and Juliana were singing their climactic final number, " 'Til Death." Since the audience was in complete darkness, I couldn't discern faces. So I was forced to stand there, behind all the cheering fans, watching the star-crossed duo sing their long and brassy duet, before finally falling on top of each other's sword-shaped microphones.

Okay, stop clapping so we can get to that damn finale.

"Ladies and gentlemen," announced the actor portraying the sexy/sinister emcee. "As you can see, our two finalists are . . . disqualified. Everybody say, 'Boo-hoo!' "

"Boo-hoo!"

"But listen up, people! This dark and tragic cloud has a solid-gold lining! One of you, yes, you, will be chosen as the next . . . idol of Verona! Houselights!"

As usual, the audience went wild. It was a tough task—scanning this collection of screaming faces and waving arms for two slender soap stars. *Maybe he'll choose Nate or Jenna as the idol. He loves to pick celebrities.*

Suddenly, the emcee straightened his dancer's body, made his mouth into a tight O.

The crowd completely lost it; they knew what was coming next. Most of them began stomping their feet or clapping in unison.

You'd think that outfit of Nate's would reflect the light.

"The judges have made their selection. All the Capulets, all the Montagues have cast their votes. And the waiting is over. The next idol of Verona is"—he paused for a packed moment—"someone who's already a star!"

Thank you.

"The most fabulous fan we know, profiled in this week's *New Yorker* . . . Tabitha Meeks! Come on up, Tabs!"

Oh, great.

As Tabitha approached the stage, I looked for Nate's face in the crowd, running my gaze across every row, until finally I picked out Jenna's gold chignon. She was sitting at the center of row three, next to an empty seat. *He never showed. He lied to me.*

"I've never been chosen before," Tabitha said. "This is the best night of my life." As I started to leave the theater, she started singing " 'Til Death" in a voice so bell-like, so strong, that even from the beginning I knew it would be her version— not Corky's or Juliana's—that this audience would remember for the rest of their lives. *A star is born.*

I couldn't help it, I felt a little jealous. Not of Tabitha's startling voice or how she glowed under the kliegs, not of the way the entire audience jumped to their feet and cheered before she'd even finished the song—but because tonight really *was* the best night of her life. And for me, it was turning out to be the worst.

I was on the sidewalk trying to hail another cab when I heard a female voice behind me. "You've got some nerve, bitch."

I spun around. Under a streetlight stood Jenna, her skin smooth and beige as a mannequin's, her eyes bright with anger. *This is all I need.*

"Excuse me?" I said.

"I said, 'You've got some—'"

"By 'excuse me,'" I said between my teeth, "I didn't mean, 'What?' I meant, 'Why?'—a.k.a. '*Why* are you assaulting me?' a.k.a., '*Why* don't you go away?'"

"You're having an affair with him, and don't try to deny it," she said. "And in case you even care, he's being treated for chronic sex addiction. So you're not only a slut; you're an enabler."

I had a near-desperate urge to punch her in the face, but I managed to refrain. "Jenna," I said, as quietly as I could, "I am not sleeping with Nate. I have a boyfriend. And even if I didn't have a boyfriend and Nate didn't have a girlfriend, I still wouldn't sleep with Nate."

"You might have everybody else fooled with the heroic-schoolteacher act, but not me. You're nothing more than a sympathy vulture!"

"I swear to God, if you weren't Ezra's mom I'd do you such physical damage right now—"

"Listen, sweetheart. I know how to run a recent search history on a computer."

I stared at her. "So?"

"I know he Googled you. And I know he went to see you because I found dark brown hairs on his shirt. And he called me Sam during sex. He didn't think I heard him, but I did."

"First of all, those weren't my hairs."

"Well, whose were—"

"You have to ask him."

"You expect me to believe—"

"Second, he did come and see me, at Sunny Side for his idiotic twelve-step thing. To ask for my forgiveness so he could move on. That's all. If you don't believe me, you can talk to Terry. Or the other teacher, Veronica."

"But—"

"Third, do you have any idea how many Sams—male and female—Nate could have been referring to?! I mean, Christ, he doesn't even call me Sam! He calls me Samantha!"

Jenna visibly cringed. "Shit. He *does*, doesn't he?"

"Fourth, I am having a really terrible night right now, mainly because my boyfriend also seems to think I'm sleeping with Nate, so I just don't need any more—"

"Oh, God. I . . ."

"What?"

"I think I might have jumped to conclusions."

"You *think*?"

"I . . . I . . . don't know what's wrong with me. It's probably the soap. All that insanity and drama every day. I'm too much in character as Blythe. Too deeply in the moment . . ."

I sighed. "Nate has a way of making real life into a soap opera, doesn't he?"

She nodded.

"Sorry he stood you up tonight. But I'll tell you what—he really, really doesn't want to lose you."

"Hey," Jenna said. "Can we just . . . like . . . take two? Pretend I never acted like a horrible bitch to you and talk about—I don't know—Ezra?"

"Sure." A cab turned onto our street. "You want that?" I asked her.

"You take it. My limo's picking me up."

As the cab edged closer and pulled to a stop, I saw the ad with Sydney's face. I wished I could "take two" on today, at least.

Krull had to be home by now. Maybe he'd be sitting in front of the TV, watching replays of some Yankees game, unable to go to bed for worry, with Jake sleeping in his lap. I would walk in and turn off the TV. "Talk about not giving me a chance to explain," I would say. And I'd tell him everything Nate had said to me outside the restaurant.

Then Krull would understand why I'd lied to him—after all, my ex's "whole fucking life" was on the line—so he'd promise to be discreet when he called Nate in for questioning. And we could go back to that distant, soft-focus past of five hours ago.

Maybe he'd let me know what he'd been trying to tell me over dinner, maybe not. It didn't matter. All I wanted to do was glue the two of us back together.

On the ride back, the cab driver said, "Anybody ever tell you you look like Sydney Stark-Leiffer?"

"Yeah."

"Hey, it's a compliment. She's hot."

I rolled my eyes.

"I'd put her show on, but my radio's fucked up."

"She's a terrible mother." I hadn't even been thinking that—not in those words, at least.

"Really? Man, you'd never know it. She's always talking about her daughter, how close they are."

"Bullshit!"

"Jeez. Mellow out."

We didn't say anything for the rest of the ride. I even paid in silence, let him keep the change. *Serves me right for taking another cab. I can't afford to take cabs all the time. Who do I think I am, anyway? Sydney Stark-take-cabs-everywhere-stay-at-the-fucking-Plaza-get-three-face-lifts-a-year-and-love-your-hairdresser-more-than-your-daughter-Leiffer?*

But she wasn't worth thinking about.

I'll go into that apartment and say, "First of all, I'm sorry for not telling you the truth in the first place. . . ."

By the time the elevator doors opened on our floor, I'd rehearsed everything I was going to say to Krull, from start to finish.

I sprinted down the hall, practically throwing my key into the lock. But when I opened the door to our apartment, I saw nothing but darkness inside, heard no baseball play-offs, no TV at all— just the thud of Jake's paws on the floor and a hoarse, hungry "Meh."

I turned on the lights, then poured Jake a bowl of dry food and some water. "Hello?"

No answer, and even before I did a quick walk-through of the small apartment on the chance Krull might have passed out in some remote corner of it, I knew I was alone.

He would've fed Jake, for one thing.

I saw the three Sterling roses he'd given me. I'd placed them in a vase on the kitchen counter. One for "I," one for "love," one for "you."

The cordless receiver was still lying on the floor, its tiny battery pack hanging out, attached to wires thin as nerves.

I walked over—just stared at it for a few minutes, the same way you'd stare at a dying animal on your lawn. *Should I try to save it, or just clean it up?*

I restored the batteries to their proper position, then found the plastic cover and snapped it back on. Nothing else was missing, so I brought it back to the base and recharged for a lot longer than usual.

And, sure enough, when I put the receiver to my ear, I heard the dial tone.

"Fixable," I said to no one.

Back in January, Yale and Peter had given me a bottle of twelve-year-old, single-malt Scotch for my twenty-ninth birthday. Knowing how much I appreciated the really good stuff, they'd practically gone into debt to buy it, saving up Peter's tips and cooking their own meals for well over two months.

When I'd opened the package, I'd gone speechless for a good minute and vowed not to break the gold seal until I honestly had something to celebrate.

But at eleven p.m., with no one in this apartment to keep me company but Jake and the couple next door (who, I swear, had been fighting for the past half hour about a *grocery bill*), that seal was looking very breakable.

"I didn't ask for turnips! Why did you buy turnips?"

"You said turnips!"

"I said *parsley!*"

"Well, fuck you, you got turnips now!"

At least they have each other. The fact that I'd actually had this thought was enough to make me crack the seal and pour myself a huge glass, straight up, without feeling a shred of guilt over it.

I took a long swallow. It was smooth and warm going down—and with a slight thrill to it—nothing like any Scotch I'd ever had—even Black Label. It made me mad I'd consumed so much cheap wine at the Indian place, because that had surely numbed my palate before this singular experience, and God, I was so lonely it hurt. Where was Krull?

"What the hell is this?"

"Marshmallow fluff."

"What?"

"Marshmallow fluff, motherfucker!"

Before I could fully comprehend what I was doing—which, for the record, was getting shit-faced alone in my apartment—I'd drained the entire glass and was pouring myself another.

"I'm taking your churchin' credit card!"

"You take my credit card, I take your fuckin' balls!"

"You took those long ago, honey!" I couldn't believe I had just said that—actually, *shrieked* was more accurate. Drinking and screaming alone in my apartment. Joining in on other people's domestic disturbances. "And what the hell is churching?" I continued. "Speak English, asshole!"

I clamped my hand over my mouth. Jake had come out of the kitchen, and seemed to be staring at me as if I'd gone insane.

"Cut it out. At least I fed you."

I noticed a sudden quiet all around me, and wondered if my neighbors weren't calling the cops, whispering into their phone about the crazy, screaming bitch next door. Wouldn't that be ironic?

I walked back into the bedroom and put an ear up to the wall, but still I heard nothing. No phone calls. Maybe I'd actually embarrassed them into shutting up.

Jake jumped up on Krull's empty side of the bed. I sat down next to him, petting him until he purred, loud as a little outboard motor. "At least you still like me."

The cordless receiver was on the bed, next to Jake; I'd been carrying it around like a security blanket. And without another thought, I picked it up, hit redial, and was immediately connected with my mother's producer. "Dr. Sydney's 'Art of Caring' on WLUV," said the polished, professional voice. "Please tell me your name, and what you'd like to talk to Dr. Stark-Leiffer about."

"She's not a doctor."

"Pardon?"

"Uh . . . my name is . . . Sarah Flannigan."

"Only first names are necessary."

"Sorry. Sarah. And what I'd like to talk to . . . the doctor about is . . ." My voice sounded wet and choked. I clenched both fists. *Don't cry. . . .* "I feel abandoned."

"By whom, Sarah?"

"Everyone. My boyfriend—"

"You will be the next caller. Turn off your radio if it's on. Dr. Stark-Leiffer will be with you after the commercial break."

"Shit, she will?"

All I got in response was a man's voice, telling listeners how they could be debt-free within thirty days.

I took a deep, shivering breath. *What am I going to say to her? Am I really going to tell my mother off, live on the air?*

Is this going to make her lose her job?

Next thing I knew, I was listening to Sydney's piped-in voice—soft and gentle, the same voice she used to read me bedtime stories as a kid. "Welcome back to Dr. Sydney's 'Art of Caring,'" she said, "I care about you."

I was about to hang up when I heard, "Next up, we have Sarah from Manhattan. Sarah, what can I help you with?"

This is so weird.

"Sarah? Honey?"

Finally, I got my jaw working. "I . . . I'm calling because . . . my boyfriend left, and I don't know where he is."

A long pause. *She recognizes my voice. Why didn't I use a fake accent? I should have—*

"Did you have a fight?"

"Yes. And no."

"What do you mean, yes and no?" Sydney didn't seem rattled, didn't sound like she knew me as anything other than another one of her fucked-up fans.

"Sarah, are you still there? I said—"

"I know what you said." I coughed. "We didn't have an actual fight because there was no yelling. He never yells."

"And you consider fighting to be yelling at each other."

"Yes."

"Fair enough. Do you ever yell?"

"Sometimes." I exhaled. "For instance, I just yelled at my neighbors."

Another pause. "Why don't you tell me what happened between you and your boyfriend."

"I didn't tell him the truth about something."

"Was it important that he know the truth?"

"Isn't it always important to know the truth?"

"No."

"That's your actual answer? Just, 'No'? In other words, you're saying lying is great."

"Not great. But sometimes the best option."

"You mean, like, how it says on your press materials you're forty-five years old?"

She laughed. "Touché."

"Touché?!"

"Sarah, can I ask you a question?"

"Ummm . . ."

"When my daughter was five years old, she asked if her daddy was a good man. You think I should have told her the truth?"

Daddy is good, and he loves you very much.

"What do you mean?"

"I don't know whether you've read my books or not, but my daughter's daddy left us when she was a teeny little kid."

"I'm familiar with that story."

"I understand he'd gotten all he needed from me. But my daughter. Not once did he try to contact her. Never sent her a letter, not a card for her birthday. Nothing."

Look, Sammy-bear, your daddy sent you a birthday card. Isn't that nice?

"He called once when she was ten. Asking for money. I said, 'I won't give you a dime, but would you like to know how your daughter is doing?' He hung up the phone after I said I wouldn't give him a dime. Does that sound like a good man to you, Sarah? Should I have told my daughter about that phone call?"

"He . . . didn't . . . send her cards?"

"Not a nineteen-cent postcard, Sarah. Not a chain letter."

Dear Sammy, I wish I could be with you for your birthday, but I hope you like this pony card. (Your mommy told me you love ponies!)

"That's . . ."

"But I bought her some cards. Did it four, five years in a row. Because I figured she should at least get a birthday card from her father. Was that wrong, Sarah? Should I have told her that I'd bought the cards myself?"

You're my most special girl and I love you. Love, Daddy.

"He . . . didn't love . . . your daughter. Did he?"

"Who knows?" Then her voice got softer. "I'm sure he did love her. In his own way."

"What the hell kind of way is—"

"What I'm trying to say is, there's a reason why people talk about 'brutal honesty.' If we all told nothing but the truth, all the time, the suicide rate would triple. There's so much vulnerable, fragile equipment inside human beings. It's why we have skin, and it's why we build up emotional layers, too. There's nothing wrong with protecting yourself. And there's nothing wrong with protecting someone you love."

I closed my eyes. "I wasn't protecting anyone I love," I said. "I lied to my boyfriend because . . . somebody else asked me to . . . to keep a secret."

"Would it hurt anyone for you to keep the secret?"

All we talked about was Live and Let Live. *I didn't even know her last name. . . . Just give me twenty-four hours. . . .* "I don't think so."

"Then your boyfriend has to learn that you are not an open book. This may surprise you, but there are probably lots of things about him that *you* don't know."

I stared at the ceiling. "It doesn't."

"Doesn't what?"

"Surprise me."

"Let me ask you something, Sarah. You said earlier that your boyfriend doesn't ever yell at you?"

"Yes."

"But you yell at him."

"Sometimes. Not that often, but . . ."

"You know why people yell?"

"Ummm . . . because they're angry?"

"Because they want to be heard, Sarah. Do you want to be heard?"

"Yes." I felt a tear trickling down my cheek. "Yes, I do."

"All human beings want to be heard. All of us want to be understood, to be valued, don't we?"

"Yes."

"If we're not heard, we either scream at the top of our lungs, or we shut up completely. And both feel terrible, don't they?"

"Yes . . . yes, they do."

"Well, let me tell you something, Sarah. *I hear you.*"

"You don't even know who I am."

"Yes, I do, honey," she said. "Yes, I do."

And I started sobbing. I couldn't help myself. I hung up the phone without saying good-bye to Dr. Sydney—to my mother—who had just spent more time talking about me, and only me, than I could ever remember her doing in my life.

And she didn't even know who I was.

I kept crying until my whole face was wet and my muscles went lax and there was nothing left inside me but air. And then, without knowing it, I fell asleep.

Lying in bed, I heard the key in the door, heavy footsteps in the living room ... *thump, thump, thump.*

Well, it's about time.

I wondered if I should let Krull know I was awake. Maybe confront him in the living room, ask why he hadn't trusted me. *How can he have evidence? What the hell was he talking about?*

I inhaled sharply. *Actually, I think it would be a better idea if I pretend to be asleep.*

Thump, thump, thump ...

He was making more noise than usual. No ninja-lawman routine this time. He wanted to be heard. For him, this was yelling.

I was aware of him now, moving past the bed, opening the closet door, working the combination on the safe. Why didn't I know that combination, anyway?

Thirteen-thirteen-thirteen.

Is that it, really?

I sat up in bed, opened my eyes and saw him hunched over the safe. He wasn't taking off his gun; he was putting something inside.

"Hiding a present from me?" I said.

Krull turned around. His hair was sopping wet from rain, and drops rested on his nose and cheeks. He smiled broadly. "You bet I am!"

He threw Nate Gundersen's severed head in my lap.

"What did you do?" I said. But the tone of my voice was strange; it didn't fit the situation. "Tell me what you did right now, John Gabriel Krull," I said, like I was scolding a student. My "voice of authority."

The phone started ringing. "Telephone!" Krull said cheerfully. It kept ringing and ringing.

I wrenched my eyes open. *Dreaming, thank God that was a dream, thank—*

Riiing. I looked at the pillow next to mine, then the clock. It was six a.m. The phone was ringing, and I was still alone in the bed. But the closet door was open.

Riiing.

I reached down beside me and grabbed the cordless receiver off the floor. The caller ID screen read PRIVATE NUMBER. "Hello?"

"Sam . . ." It took me a few moments to identify the voice, choked as it was with tears, with panic.

"Yale? Are you—"

"Please come to the theater now," the voice said. "And bring John. Oh, God . . . *please!*"

Yale's cell phone went to static before I could ask what was going on.

Still in the clothes I'd been wearing the night before, I slipped on a pair of flip-flops, ran down the hall, rode the elevator downstairs and took a cab to the Space.

I saw him sitting on the curb out in front. Dressed to rehearse in a leotard top and sweats, he was rocking back and forth with his arms grasping his stomach, as if he were literally trying to hold himself together.

Yale's face was pale and wet, and when I put my arms around him, I could feel his whole body trembling. *In shock.*

"Where's John?"

"I don't know."

"What's that supposed to mean?"

"What happened, Yale?"

He didn't reply, but he did stand up. This was something of a strange relief—knowing he at least had that much strength in him. Then he said, "Peter's guarding the door."

I followed him through the courtyard to the theater. Peter stood out front, staring, his usually olive complexion a bloodless white. "Where's John?" he said.

"She doesn't fucking know."

"All right," I said, as slowly and calmly as possible. "Why do you guys think you need John?"

Wordlessly, Peter opened the theater door.

The first thing I noticed was how bright it was in the theater. Every houselight was up, every worklight backstage, every klieg on the catwalk, blazing. *Why?* I started to mention it—but then I noticed the next thing.

Facedown, stage center, was the body of a man, blood pooling out beneath him like a slick red mat.

"Who is that?"

"We have absolutely no idea," said Yale. "We just unlocked the theater, and saw all the lights on and . . . him."

I took a deep breath, steadied myself. "Okay. We need to call the police."

"That's why we wanted you to bring John," Peter said.

I moved closer to the body. "Either of you guys have a cell phone that works?"

I didn't bring mine," said Peter. "Yale called, and I ran." He was wearing shorts and an I ♥ QUE-BEC T-shirt, both inside out.

Yale said, "My battery died."

"That's all right." I moved closer, until I was standing directly in front of the stage. "We can call from the box office."

The body looked to have been stabbed repeatedly in the back, and there was so much blood I couldn't even tell the hair color.

"Okay. The important thing to remember is not to touch him, and . . ." Suddenly, I felt myself stop, as if the rest of the sentence had somehow gotten lodged in my throat and I might never speak again.

Clutched in the dead man's hand was a fresh Sterling rose.

"Do you think he was killed here, in the theater?" said Yale.

"I . . . don't know."

"Who do you think he was?" Peter said. "A fan?"

Slowly, I nudged his face away from the stage.

"Sam, you said you're not supposed to—"

His eyes were open and vacant as two huge, black marbles. His mouth was open too, in some kind of final, silent scream. It was hard to imagine that overpriced accent coming out of this mouth, hard to imagine these blue, bloodless lips, tightening elegantly around an O.

"He was," I said.

Peter said, "He was what?"

"A fan. He was a fan."

9

Six Charlie

There's a definite choreography to crime-scene response; I'd come to learn this in the past year and a half. I say *choreography* rather than *system* because it is, in its way, a sad kind of dance, repeated over and over again with the exact same steps, no matter what the circumstances may be.

For instance: This man needed paramedics just about as much as he needed ice-skating lessons, yet sure enough, EMS arrived within minutes of our 911 call.

And, as they set about determining that the stiff, cold man lying in a pool of his own blood was, in fact, dead, the sector car showed up.

Staying on script, the two uniformed cops from the sector car (Sector Six Charlie in this case;

precinct sectors patrolled by squad cars get alpha-
betical pseudonyms, like army platoons) began
preliminary questioning of the witnesses. They
asked Yale, Peter and me for our full names, ages
and occupations—even though, in my case, they
knew the answers to all three of those questions.

Even though there were so many other questions more relevant: Why this man? Why the
rose? Why this theater?

I remembered the broken Sterling rose in front
of Marla's shrine, the bloody valentine heart finger-
painted on the brick wall I used to love. HE KILLED
MARLA S. DON'T GET HIM ANGRY AGAIN.

Were two people really murdered because of
me? Two people stabbed to death, their corpses
placed where I could see them? If that was true,
then why?

"I don't know his name. But he's planning . . ." The
man was lying dead, center stage at the theater
where I worked. He would never be able to complete that sentence.

"Did any of you know the victim?" asked one
of the sector cops—a blunt-speaking redhead
named Fiona Hamilton.

"I did," I said.

Her partner, Billy Rathke, asked, "What was
his name?"

"I have no idea. Can you guys please get Boyle
and Patton over here?"

"Sure," said Fiona. "But what about John?"

"If you can find him, that would be great."

After Billy phoned the Crime Scene Unit from his cell and Fiona relayed facts to the detective squad room on the car radio, they asked us a few more basic questions. Who had found the body initially? Why were we here so early? How long did it take us to call the police?

Who did this? That was the question I needed answered.

CSU arrived on cue with their surgical gloves and cameras, their ominous dark briefcases packed with sterile evidence bags. I wanted to follow CSU into the theater—if only to look at the victim once more—but I was just a civilian witness; my place was outside.

So I sat down on the squad car's bumper, closed my eyes, went over what little I'd learned from eavesdropping on Six Charlie:

Someone had repeatedly shoved a long, sharp knife into the man's back. Most likely, it was a hunting knife, like the one Nate had posed with on the cover of *Soap Opera Digest*. And like the as-yet-unfound knife used to murder Marla Soble.

Though he'd been attacked from behind, there was some sign of a struggle. Scratches on his hands and impact wounds on his elbows and forearms indicated he'd fought back for an unusually long time before ultimately going unconscious from blood loss.

In other words, this guy may not have seen his killer coming, but he sure as hell knew what was going on. *Watch your back.*

He had not been killed in the theater. The man's body showed signs of postmortem bruising—secondary lividity—meaning that, like Marla Soble, he'd been picked up and moved to a significant spot. It was important to the killer for this body to be discovered. Here.

The number of knife wounds on the man had not yet been determined—he was too much of a bloody mess, necessitating closer inspection by CSU—but I'd have bet both my salaries on thirteen. Just like Marla.

Same weapon, same killer—only Marla had gotten it in the chest, while this man had been stabbed in the back.

Mirror images, killed because . . . *Because you made someone angry.*

Yale sat down next to me and handed me a bottle of water. "Want it? I got it from the paramedics."

"Thanks."

"Peter's throwing up right now—"

"Sorry," Billy interrupted. "But you can't converse with each other until you're released from questioning."

Yale leveled his eyes at him. "Billy, right? I met

you at John and Sam's Christmas party. You were dancing to that fabulous ABBA song in your underwear? I didn't know they made Spiderman briefs for grown men!"

Billy's face went pink. "Go ahead and talk."

"Thank you." He turned to me. "It's not fair, Sam."

"What's not fair?"

"This. You should be happy, or bored, or annoyed or whatever the rest of us humans are." He put his arm around me. "You've already used up your lifetime supply of mortal terror."

"The man in the theater . . . he knew, Yale. He tried to warn me, and now he's . . ."

He's angry.

"You didn't know. How were you supposed to?"

"I'm just such a . . . crappy judge of character." Even as I said it, a string of thoughts flooded my mind. Ugly thoughts, lodged in my subconscious, but now center stage. Like the dead body.

Krull handing me three Sterling roses. *"One for 'I,' one for 'love,' one for 'you.' "*

The bent rose in front of Marla's shrine, the rose clasped in the dead man's bloody hand.

Krull, climbing into bed after a four-hour disappearance, his hair wet, his skin wet. *"Sorry. I just needed time alone."*

"He's taking this case too personally," Pierce had

said. *"There's something else going on in his head about Soble."*

HE KILLED MARLA S. DON'T GET HIM ANGRY AGAIN.

"The only him I got angry that night . . . was you!" How had he looked at me when I said that? What was that strange emotion sneaking into his eyes?

"What would you do if you found out something about me? Something that . . . isn't good?"

"Sam?" said Yale. "Are you okay?"

"Yeah . . . I'm just . . . I'm exhausted. . . ." *If it's the beginning of the end when you suspect your lover of cheating, what does it mean when you're afraid he might have . . .*

"Touch anything?" said Billy.

"Huh?"

"I forgot to ask if you guys touched anything at the crime scene. CSU wants to know."

"Just the body," I said.

"What?!"

"I only lifted his head for a couple of seconds. I just needed to see his face."

Fiona left the car. "Hey, Yale, is your man still busy puking?"

While Yale went back to the phalanx of parked ambulances to check, she said, "The bad news is, we're going to drive you guys to the precinct house for questioning."

"And the good news?"

She smiled. "The good news is, you get to talk to John."

"You found him?" I said.

"Sure. It's not like I had to issue an all-points bulletin or anything."

"Not yet."

"What?"

"Nothing."

Yale, Peter and I climbed into the back of the squad car, and the choreography continued. In five or ten minutes, the medical examiner would make his grand entrance in that dark blue morgue van with the sad white letters stenciled on the side.

But we wouldn't be around for that. We wouldn't be around to see this broken little man—the star of this show—carried out of the theater in a body bag.

When we got to the squad room, Fiona and Billy took our driver's licenses and led us into two separate interview rooms for questioning. Fiona stayed with me; Billy and another male uniform went with Yale and Peter. Same-sex chaperones, as if a strip search were involved in questioning.

The interview room was small and shabby— they all were, which had always struck me as counterproductive. Honestly, who wants to answer questions in a place like that, with one metal table, folding chairs that hurt your ass to look at them—not to mention that big spy window, masquerading as a mirror but fooling no one?

Besides, what was I supposed to say? *"I've got a sneaking suspicion my boyfriend—that's right, your medal-winning superhero detective—might have . . ."*

I couldn't even think it all the way through, let alone say it out loud. *You're tense, you're scared, you're hungover, so cut it out, because he wouldn't. John Krull would not.*

Then who would?

"Hey, Fiona, do you know if they ever got a match on the fingerprints from Marla's apartment?"

"Which ones?"

"The valentine."

"Oh, ewww, yeah . . . There aren't any."

"But he finger painted that thing."

"Gloves. We're talking very thin, plastic, sterile *gloves*. Like a surgeon would use."

My mind flashed to CSU. "Or like a cop might use? To collect evidence?"

"Exactly."

I dug my fingernails into the palms of my hands. *Stop it.*

"You want to know the freakiest thing about that heart, though?"

I nodded.

"It wasn't her blood."

"What?"

"It's not Marla's DNA. Tests came up negative for both her and her fiancé. We're running the sample through all the unsolved-crime databases, and the felon database too. So we'll find out soon, I guess. . . ."

"That's so . . ."

"Isn't it? Maybe we've got a cutter, but I don't know. . . . All the cutters I've ever known have been girls. And this one definitely seems like a man."

"Why?"

"The removal and posing of the body. And the overkill. Those are usually guy things. Fucked-up, angry guy things."

Look at me, Sam. I'm a man. Do you think violence is a part of my DNA?

"Stop," I whispered.

"Stop what?"

"Nothing, Fi. You got an aspirin, by any chance?"

"I'll get you one out of the first-aid box. Just a sec." She opened the door. "Oh, hi, Detective Krull," she said.

He was clean-shaven, his hair damp from a recent shower, and he wore a dark blue suit I'd never seen before. "Where did you get those clothes?" I said.

"I keep a spare suit in my locker."

"Well, that makes a million and one things you've never told me about." Angry as I was, though, it was still so good to see him.

My perspective came back, and those awful thoughts crumbled as I watched him, watched my sexy, flawed but incredibly sweet John Krull say, "I'm so sorry, Sam."

He was not, could never be, a killer.

Fiona quietly placed two aspirins on the table, then mumbled something about the other witness interviews and crept back out of the room.

I aimed my eyes at Krull and took a deep breath. "You left me in the restaurant without giving me a chance to explain, and that wasn't fair."

"I know."

"You left me alone all night long, and it isn't the first time."

"I know."

"You're the one with the secrets—not me! You're the one with the . . . the moods and the . . . who knows what the hell you're thinking three-quarters of the time because—"

"I know."

"You need to realize that I'm not an open book, and I yell because I want to be heard!"

"I know, Sam, I know."

He put both arms around me and held me, and just like always, I felt so protected, so safe.

I closed my eyes, inhaling the clean scent of his skin. My boyfriend, who had too many secrets but wasn't a murderer. Who disappeared so much, but was here now. And that, I supposed, was better than nothing.

I kissed his mouth. *Cigarettes.*

"Where were you?" I said. "I drank all this Scotch, and I yelled at the neighbors. I even called my mother."

"I'm so sorry."

"And then . . . then this . . ."

"I know. I should have been there for you."

"And . . . what was this evidence you were talking about?"

"Oh, that woman, Jenna Sargent."

I looked up at him. "What about her?"

"She came over here two days ago, told me you were screwing Nate. She said she found these straight brown hairs on his shirt and I could run DNA tests on them."

"Man, she has been on that soap too long."

"Anyway, it's bullshit, because I remembered—you said he visited you at school. So of course your hair could've gotten on him, even if he leaned against a wall or brushed against your chair."

"It wasn't even my hair, John. It was—"

"Yes, it was."

I pulled away from him. "You ran the test?"

"Well . . . yeah. Of course."

I backed up, stared at his face.

"What difference does a test make if you've got nothing to hide? You flunked it, and I still trust you. What does that say?"

"It says we don't know each other as well as I thought."

"Oh, come on," he said. It wasn't until he moved farther away that I noticed the deep, red cuts on both his hands.

We sat at the metal table in silence. "Where the hell is everybody else?" I said.

Krull pulled a pack of Marlboro Reds out of his coat pocket. "Do you mind?"

"No. Just give me the butt afterward so I can take a saliva sample."

"Sam."

"Maybe there isn't some stalker out there. Maybe it's just been you . . . staking me out."

"That's not funny."

"Tell me something. How come it's not okay for me to ask what you happen to be thinking about but it's fine for you to run secret forensic tests on me?"

He lit his cigarette. "I'm sorry. I . . . we were going through a rough patch, and Jenna Sargent tells me this crazy story. I just wanted to make sure." He looked up at the ceiling for a few seconds. "Maybe I was being such a jerk, I figured it would be a miracle if you *weren't* cheating on me."

I shook my head, but still, I felt my reserve softening a little. "Can I have a cigarette?"

As he gave me one, I couldn't take my eyes off those shimmering wounds.

"What happened to your hands?"

"Bar fight."

"Bar fight?"

But before either of us could say another word, the door opened ". . . Peter Steele is USDA *Prime,*" Fiona was saying, as Patton and Boyle entered behind her.

"Yeah, well, put your tongue back in your mouth," Patton said. "He grazes on the other pasture." She spotted Krull. "Hi, John."

"Mandy."

"So long as we're in the interview room, you mind telling me where the fuck you were for three hours yesterday? I was actually worried about you."

He's heard that one before.

"Kids," said Boyle, "we've got a case here to discuss."

"I had some personal issues," said Krull. "I know it was irresponsible and I'll make it up to you, but I'd rather talk about this . . . body . . . if you don't mind."

Fiona flipped on the tape recorder. "Please state your full name and date of birth."

"Samantha Elizabeth Leiffer. January seventh, 1973." I smiled at Boyle. "Capricorn."

"Best of the best. Hardest-working sign in the zodiac."

Fiona asked if I recognized the man's body immediately upon seeing it in the theater.

"I had to look at his face first," I said. "But then I did. Immediately." It was hard to explain the complex relationship I'd managed to form with this man I'd known for only two days, whom I'd spoken to twice, whom I'd seen alive once, and whose name I never knew. But I tried. "I don't think there's been a minute since I met him that he hasn't at least been in the back of my mind," I said.

After I was finished, I took a drag off the cigarette. It felt like someone stuffing burning cotton down my throat; never could get used to smoking, much as I tried sometimes.

"We can tell you his name now," Boyle said. "Nikolas Stavros, DOB seven/five/seventy-eight Brussels, Belgium. Father, deceased, owned a gas station, and his mother is—"

"Katia Stavros," I said.

"Yes."

Krull said, "Who is that?"

"She is the super of a walk-up right across from Sunny Side," I said.

"If it was her son watching Sam with the binoculars," Boyle said, "it would explain why she didn't say anything to us about—"

Krull said, "He was watching you—"

I rolled the dead cigarette butt between my fingers. "Maybe he was trying to keep me safe."

There was a knock on the door. Fiona opened it for Pierce. "Hi, Detective."

Patton said, "There's not a bomb in the squad room, is there?"

Boyle guffawed, while Fiona stifled a giggle.

Pierce's eyes narrowed. "That's not funny, Patton."

"Ah, lighten up," said Krull. "I was there too, remember?"

Pierce cracked a smile. "Sure, John." He winked at Boyle. "Guy buys me a twelve-pack, he can ask to diddle my dead mom and I'll say sure. Oops. Sorry, ladies."

Boyle rubbed his temples. "You got some questions for Sam?"

"Just one," Pierce said. "How you holding up?"

I smiled. "Not bad, considering."

Pierce smiled back. He had a kind smile. If it wasn't for that gleaming head of his, I imagined he could be a very comforting presence during difficult interrogations.

Boyle said, "Only one more from me, Sam. This series of messages you received . . . 'You are in danger. Don't show this to him, you got him angry, he's always watching you . . .' Do you have any idea who this *him* might be?"

I shot a quick look at Krull, and his gaze went down to the wounds on his hands. *Is that a bite mark?*

"Yes," I said. "I do have an idea."

Patton said, "Who?"

Funny what love does. Your boyfriend gets in some so-called bar fight and winds up with bite marks on his hands. And strange as you think that sounds, much as you try to plaster warning signs all over your brain, all you really want to do is put Band-Aids on those wounds—make him feel better.

"I think," I said, "it's an obsessed fan—someone who got interested in me when I was in the news."

"Someone you don't know."

I glanced at Krull again. "Someone I've never met."

Nothing stirs up claustrophobia more than a half hour in an interview room. So when Boyle declared the questioning session over, it wasn't a second too soon. On my way out, as Fiona brushed by to reconnect with her partner, I took a huge, gulping breath of the air her movement created, then exhaled shakily.

Patton said, "You okay?"

"I'm fine. I just . . . I want to get out of this place." I looked from her face, to Krull's, to Boyle's, to Pierce's. "Can I?"

"You're late for your class, huh?" said Krull.

I nodded.

"I don't see why she can't go to work," said Boyle. "So long as we put her under surveillance."

I glared at Krull. "That wouldn't be anything new."

"I promise I'll never do that again."

"Do what again?" said Pierce.

However Krull might have replied, he was interrupted by a group of three uniforms escorting a woman into the squad room. She was smaller than me, with short silver hair, powder-blue sweatpants, and an oversize T-shirt that read, in childlike letters, #1 GRANDMA.

She looked as if she'd been crying for a very long time.

The cops were taking her into an interview room, but in the seconds before she entered, she turned toward our group. Her expression was flat, numb—but then something happened.

The woman's bloodshot eyes widened, and her face began to twitch, as if she were trying to breathe, but had suddenly forgotten how.

"You . . ." she whispered. Then she collapsed into sobs. A female officer put her arms around the tiny woman, nearly lifting her away, out of our sight, into the safety of the interview room.

"Who was that?" I asked.

"Katia," Patton said quietly. "Katia Stavros."

10

Monsters and Superheroes

Had he not been found in my theater with a Sterling rose in his hand, there could easily have been another explanation for Nikolas Stavros's murder, as it turned out. He was a crack dealer who had spent eight months on Riker's Island back in 2000 and "may have fallen back into crime" from time to time, his mother claimed.

He was also Mrs. Stavros's youngest son—a smart, kindhearted boy who had simply gotten involved with the wrong crowd after his family moved to America and his father had died, unexpectedly, of a heart attack.

"Another screwed-up kid with a missing dad," I said, after the sector cops who'd picked her up told us her story.

Krull just looked at me.

"Yeah, well, Mrs. Stavros's other three sons are in Greece, and she says she's gonna move there ASAP," said a mustachioed sector cop, Brandyberry. "She says America is bad luck, and who can blame her?"

"Why did she . . . react that way when she saw us?" I asked.

"I think it was Art and me," Patton said. "You know what she told us yesterday? She said she had no children. I'm sure she thought we were at her apartment to arrest Nikolas again, and that's why she said it. But . . ."

Boyle said, "I hear ya."

"What?" Pierce said.

"We're the ones she thinks are bad luck," said Boyle. "Not America."

I stared down at my feet, at the bright purple flip-flops I'd shoved on this morning when Yale had called, begging me to come to the theater. They looked stupid to me, needlessly festive against the stained gray linoleum of the squad room floor. "I'm bad luck," I said quietly. "He was killed for trying to warn me about . . ." My voice trailed off.

Krull said, "Warn you about what?"

"I don't know," I said. "That's what scares me so much. I don't know."

*   *   *

To the detectives who had briefly questioned her in the interview room before letting her go home to grieve, Katia Stavros claimed to have no idea who I was, or why Nikolas would have left me those notes.

But as we left the precinct house and stepped into the hot sun, Boyle said, "I still think she's hiding something."

"Might be," said Krull. "But who the hell wants to drag it out of her now?"

"Maybe once her son is buried and she gets a little closure, she'll come to us." Pierce looked at me. "So you're really gonna go teach a bunch of four-year-olds now?"

"I think I need to," I said.

Patton nodded. "I'm jealous."

Fiona and Billy gave me a ride to Sunny Side in their sector car, explaining on the way over that they'd be surveying the area for suspicious activity while I taught. At twelve o'clock, they'd bring me home—since the Space was now a crime scene and therefore dark. I pictured Tabitha arriving at the theater at the usual time, expecting only her regular place at the front of the line, her daily forty-dollar transaction—and seeing yellow crime-scene tape instead. *The best night of her life was the last night of someone else's.* "We are going to have some very unhappy *Idol* fans on our hands," I said.

"Hey, speaking of fans," said Fiona. "I just love your mother's radio show."

"Oh, yeah?"

"This one girl called in last night? She had problems with her boyfriend, and I swear she reached such a breakthrough. Your mom cured her!"

"I wouldn't say that."

"What do you mean?"

"Nothing. Just . . . they edit things for radio."

As I started to get out of the car, Fiona handed me a walkie-talkie. "If you need us for anything," she explained. "It beats a cell phone, 'cause there's just one button."

"Thanks, guys."

"Sam?" said Billy.

"Uh-huh?"

"Your friend . . . that gay guy."

"Yale?"

"He's not going to tell anybody about my underwear, is he? I don't think anybody else from the party remembers, and I'd like to keep it that way."

"Billy shops in the boys' department," said Fiona.

"Shut up, Fiona."

"Hey, I don't blame you," she said. "It's cheaper. If the briefs fit—"

"It's not boys; it's big-and-tall . . . *young men*, so you can just—"

"I'm sure Yale's on your side," I said. "He's like me—he's got a weakness for superheroes."

When I opened the door to my classroom, it was nearly nine a.m., and one of Veronica's assistants was teaching my kids.

"I'm so sorry," I said. "I had an emergency—"

"It's okay," said the assistant—a sweet, freckle-faced girl named either Mary or Marie—I never got it right. "But . . . um . . . Terry wants to see you in his office."

"Why?"

"Sorry, I don't know."

I heard Charlotte Weiss say, "Miss Leiffer got a time-out." And as I hurried down the hall toward Terry's office, I was well aware of Veronica peering at me through her open door. I would have told her to mind her own business, if she had any of her own business to mind.

I couldn't figure out why Terry would call me into his office instead of talking to me after school. This was the first time in my five years of teaching here that I'd shown up late without calling in. Wouldn't he assume there was a legitimate reason—a murder, for instance? Wouldn't he at least give me a chance to explain?

But when I got to the principal's office, I saw that his reasons for calling me in had nothing to do with tardiness. Terry was standing next to his desk, huddled in what appeared to be an intense conversation with Jenna Sargent.

This had better not have anything to do with my DNA. When Jenna looked up at me, though, she looked so different, it was though what she'd said in front of the Space had become a prophecy. Like we really were on "take two"—and she'd completely rewritten her role.

Jenna was wearing a plain gray sweat suit. Her face, dusted with freckles, was devoid of makeup. I noticed deep, bruiselike circles under her blue eyes. She would have looked like a pretty college student who had just put in an all-nighter, were it not for the panic that tensed the corners of her mouth, the fear she seemed to radiate.

"What's going on?" I said.

"Oh, Samantha," said Terry. "We're very, very glad you're here."

Jenna said, "I thought you'd disappeared too. A couple of days ago, I would've assumed you'd left town together. But . . . not any . . ." A tear trickled down her cheek.

Terry said, "Ms. Sargent's fiancé seems to be missing. And as he is a friend of both yours and Ezra's, it's a Sunny Side concern as well."

"For how long, Jenna? Did you ever see him last night?"

"No." She looked at me. "He was supposed to meet me at the theater. He's stood me up plenty of times, but at least he calls afterward. . . . I figured, whatever. He'll show up later with champagne and an explanation, like always. Well . . . he never showed up. He was supposed to take Ezra to school this morning. Didn't show up for that either. And Samantha, he didn't make his morning call at the studio. He always makes his . . . his . . . morning call. I looked in his dressing room and . . . and . . . God."

My eyes darted from Jenna's tearstained face to Terry's, pinched with worry, as remnants of the previous night's conversation looped through my mind like a soap opera voice-over. *I can't tell the police, Samantha. You don't understand. It will get in the papers. The fans would freak out—I could lose my job. Jenna would fucking kill me. My whole fucking life will be ruined. . . ."*

Unless he ran away, and started all over somewhere else. "Take two," I whispered.

"Pardon?" said Terry.

"Jenna," I said, "I want you to take a deep breath. In and out."

"What is this, yoga class?" She started to sob.

"I have a pretty good idea that Nate's okay."

She managed to catch her breath. "You do?"
Terry said, "Where would we find him, then?"
I looked at Jenna. "The thing is, he loves you,
but . . ."

"But?"

"But he's a huge coward . . . and I think he left
town."

"Why?"

"He had a . . ." I cleared my throat. "He . . .
flirted . . . with a woman who was later murdered, and—"

"What?!"

"He was very afraid of the scandal. Thought it
would cost him his job, and you. I said he had to
tell the police, or I'd do it for him. He asked for
twenty-four hours—to tell you, I thought. It's my
fault . . . I scared him away."

We all sat there for such a long, quiet time—
staring at the floor, our hands limp and helpless
in our laps. Until finally, Jenna said, "I'm sorry,
Sam. But I just don't think that's true."

"It is, I—"

"No, I have to agree with Ms. Sargent—that
doesn't sound right, in light of . . ." Terry turned
to Jenna. "Show her what you found. Please."

Jenna reached into her portfolio bag and removed a piece of red construction paper. I
couldn't tell what was printed on it—I could see
only the back—but I did notice that the hand

holding the paper was trembling. "See." Her voice quavered too, just like her hand. "This was in his dressing room this morning. I guess it must've come in with his fan mail, and . . . it's . . . it's . . ."

It was a collage consisting mainly of digital snapshots. Personal color photos of body parts, blood spattered, desecrated. A lifeless hand missing a thumb, a woman's bare chest riddled with stab wounds, the slim, brown back of a man obscured by dark, oozing rivulets. Straight brown hair framing a throat that had been gouged open.

At the center of the page, someone had glued Nate's *Soap Opera Digest* cover. And across the top, three words were printed huge: ALL ABOUT ME.

"This doesn't mean anything at all," I had said, in a halfhearted attempt to reassure Jenna—and myself—that Nate was okay. "But let's get the police on this anyway, just to be safe."

I'd pushed the red button on the walkie-talkie and, though Terry was surprised that our school was under surveillance for the second time in a year and a half, he still seemed happy to see Six Charlie.

They called another squad car to bring Jenna and the collage to the Twentieth Precinct, where *Live and Let Live*'s studios—and both Nate's and

Jenna's apartments—were located. When those officers arrived, I hugged her tightly and whispered, "Nate's fine," in her ear.

"How do you know?"

"I'm psychic."

We waved good-bye to Jenna. And after we heard the sirens fade, Terry said, "You are a very kind person."

It was the first compliment I'd heard him give anyone, ever. "Thank you."

Fiona and Billy asked if I felt like going home, but I said, "I need to teach my class."

"You must love those kids," Fiona said.

I did, much as anyone loves a group of children they've known for only two days. But there was another reason, too—one I wasn't as willing to admit: I didn't *want* to go home.

If someone was watching my classroom from across the street, they would have seen the kids' collages. I'd stuck them, one next to the other, on the wall facing the window. That's what I told myself as I walked down the hall to my classroom. It wasn't lost on me, though—the fact that I was actually trying to comfort myself with the idea that the murderous stalker I apparently had was not someone I knew. Was not someone who shared a closet with me, who had helped me bring magazines to school and store them in the art-supplies closet a month ago and who had, just last night, stared Nate Gundersen down. . . .

Why did my suspicions keep turning to Krull, when anyone could have killed those people, anyone could have sent Nate that collage?

The stalker asked a kid what the collages were called. That's how he knew to write, "All About Me." He asked Veronica. She's a font of information—always has been. Maybe he's related to one of my students. A sick stepfather, a schizophrenic older brother . . .

When I knocked on the door, Harry S. answered it, wearing a Cinderella costume from the dress-up bin. "I'm a princess," he said.

"Very nice."

Abraham, wearing full pirate regalia, was jabbing a toy sword at the teacher's aide Mary/Marie's legs, while Harry W. was standing on my desk in a red cape, screaming, "I'm Spider-Man!" Charlotte, also dressed as a princess—Snow White, to be exact—was happily writing her name on the wall with some kind of indelible pen, while Ida was strutting around the room in the poor teacher's aide's platform shoes.

"I'm so happy you're here," she said. "I didn't have your day planner or the keys to your art-supplies closet, so it's been like endless dress-up in here. This is a . . . very lively class you've got."

"Okay, guys, settle down!" I used the voice of authority. Everyone froze. "Ida, give the teacher

back her shoes. Charlotte, stop writing on the
wall. Abraham, Harry, calm down."

"Awesome," said Marie/Mary, and ran out the
door.

"Okay, now the good news is, everyone can
keep their dress-ups on if they want to."

"Yay!"

"The maybe not-so-good news is, no jumping
on furniture, no attacking each other or me. Everyone must sit quietly and listen to a story. . . ." I
looked around the room. "Where's Ezra?"

Ida said, "He's under your desk."

"Excuse me a minute."

I crouched down and saw Ezra, curled up into
a tiny ball in the dark space.

"What are you doing down here, honey?"

"Hiding from monsters."

"You mean Spider-Man?" I smiled. "He's not
on the desk anymore."

"Spider-Man's not a monster. He's a superhero.
Superheroes save people. Monsters take them
away." He picked at a fingernail. "Mommy
doesn't know, but I saw Uncle Nate's collage before she hid it in her purse. A monster made that."

I patted his hunched little back. "No monsters
are going to take you, honey. I won't let them."

"You a superhero?"

"As a matter of fact, I am."

A smile spread across his face. "What are your superpowers?"

"Ummm . . . I can eat ten grilled cheese sandwiches in one gulp."

He laughed. "That's silly."

"How about you?"

"I can drive the Batmobile, scale tall buildings, umm . . . Fly, for sure. Shoot lasers out of my eyes. And—"

"Scare monsters away?"

"Yes."

"Me too, Ezra. Come out from under there, and you can help me read the story, okay?"

"Oh, I forgot. I can also win Oscars."

As I helped Ezra out from under my desk, he said, "You know what? My uncle Nate forgot to take me to school today. Isn't that silly?"

I crossed my fingers behind my back. Just one set of fingers, on one hand, so the kids wouldn't notice. *He's fine. Please let him be fine.* "He was probably busy practicing his acting so he can win an Oscar," I said.

Ezra sighed dramatically. "Uncle Nate doesn't win Oscars, Miss Leiffer. He wins Daytime Emmys!"

"My mommy is gonna win a Daytime Emmy," said Charlotte.

"No, she isn't," Ezra said.

"Yes, she is!"

"Guys!"

"Miss Leiffer," Ida said.

"Uh-huh?"

"Ummm . . . We didn't spill that paint. So is it okay if we don't clean it up during cleanup time?"

"What paint, Ida?"

The little girl pointed to the closed art-supplies closet.

When I looked down at the floor, I saw what she was talking about—a puddle of dark red liquid was oozing out from under the door. "That's icky paint, all right," I whispered.

I tried taking a deep breath, but it was hard to manage breathing of any sort. *It's only paint, just spilled art supplies. Get the kids out of the room. Now.*

"Hey, everybody! Guess what time it is?"

"Story time?" said Harry S.

"Recess!"

"Yay!"

As soon as all eight kids were on the playground, I stuck my head in Veronica's classroom, where she and her two aides were helping the kids paint a giant American flag. "Can one of you guys please watch my class?" I asked.

Reluctantly, Veronica herself volunteered. As I rushed back to my classroom and slipped back in, I was vaguely aware of her calling out behind me, "Why on earth are you having recess now?"

I locked my door from the inside, grabbed the art-supply closet key from my purse, and just stared at it for a few seconds—this strange-looking key, purchased by Terry as a preventative measure last year, after my classroom had been robbed for the third time. This state-of-the-art, SAF-T brand key, like some sort of James Bond torture device—a dense, five-inch-long rectangle, with piranha teeth. *Safety.*

I unlocked the door. "It's just paint, it's just paint, it's just paint," I kept saying. It felt like a prayer.

I could hear the children's shouts wafting in from the playground, ("Gimme that!" "Whee!" "I'm Spider-Man!") as the door drifted open.

"Oh, dear God," I heard. But it was my voice. It was me standing there, alone in this room—my classroom—staring into the face of Nate Gundersen. His amber eyes were motionless, his mouth cracked open as if trapped midsentence forever. Nate's body was propped up against the shelves—amongst construction paper and glitter glue, multicolored markers and Dora the Explorer stickers—in the all-white outfit I'd seen him in, yet mostly rust-red now, from the blood that had poured out of his slashed chest, his deeply slit throat.

I looked down at his hands, alongside his feet, expecting to see Sterling roses. But what I saw instead, in his left hand, was a rolled-up piece of white construction paper. I pulled it out, unrolled it, read: *S: You kill me.* It was written in blood.

I pushed the red button on the walkie-talkie. "Come quick," I started to say. But what came out was an agonized animal sound, somewhere between a scream and a sob. It didn't seem ever to stop.

11

The Gentleman Caller

Everything started happening in snippets—
disjointed as mixed-up movie stills, or pieces of a
dream.

*Billy Rathke's cologne . . . bay rum, like my dad
used to wear.* "Keep the children outside!" *he shouts.*

"Miss Leiffer? What's wrong?" *Ezra. Just a mess,
honey. Just made a great big mess is all. Say it.
Why can't I talk?*

Fiona's voice. "Miss Leiffer's fine. Don't wor—"

Marie/Mary on her knees behind me. "Oh, God, no,
no, no, no . . ."

Billy saying, "Who is that woman? Get her out of
here."

Voices crackling out of police radios. A gust of air as

more uniforms rush by. It's got a chemical smell—a combination of polyester, metal and gun oil.

Amanda Patton's face. "Are you all right?"

Then Krull's: "Lean on me. Deep breaths. Deep . . ."

The clean smell of Krull's soap. The warmth of his arms. He didn't do this. He couldn't.

But who did? Who did this because of me?

I'm in a squad car. Don't know how I got here, where this blanket came from, but I'm cold. Could use another. I'm thinking about turning my head. . . .

S: You Kill Me

The car's moving. A woman sitting next to me, holding my hand. She must have poor circulation; her hand's like ice. Is it Patton? Must be. Who else would it be?

In the front seat, Fiona. "Where's Detective Krull?"

Patton says, "With the body."

Fiona says, "Seems like she could use him a little more than the body could."

Out the window, people on the street stop and stare in slow motion. The car is traveling fast; yet I can see the tiniest movements on each individual face.

I'm in shock. This is what shock is like. A giant magnifying glass, with freeze-frame.

Chatter drifts out of the police radio. It reminds me of the humming of bees. I can't understand any of it, except for a few words: Male. Caucasian. Morgue.

Out the window, the dark blue medical examiner's van. "He's busy today," says a cop in the front seat.

And I know what he's talking about. Two bodies in one day.

Two corpses.

I close my eyes, and I'm a twenty-one-year-old stage manager, backstage during dress rehearsal for King Lear. *He's standing inches away from me, this creation who plays Edmund the Bastard. He hasn't spoken to me during any of the earlier rehearsals, but now he's so close I can feel the heat his body emits. "I might need your help with my costume change," he says. "Is that . . . okay?"*

And then he looks at me. . . . It's like he can see through my clothes, through my skin, into my soul. He radiates. I stare back, struck silent by the heat, think-ing, That's the thing about this actor. He's 10 per-cent more alive than everybody else.

I opened my eyes to the back of Fiona's head. As I stared at her thick red hair, the disjointed, surreal feeling—the shock—began to dissipate. *Nate is dead,* I thought. *Nate Gundersen is dead.*

"How often does this ever happen?" I said, as Fiona flipped on the tape recorder. "Two murders in one day, same material witness."

Fiona said, "Not very often, I'll tell you that much." But as Boyle, Krull, Patton, Fiona and I—plus Pierce and his two partners, Munro and Sawyer—sat around the same table, Krull smok-ing the same kind of cigarette, the same strange welts on his hands, I was struck instead by how different everything was now.

No one teased Pierce about calling the bomb squad; there was no talk of astrology, no remarks coming from the women about cute male witnesses, none of the gallows humor so typical of homicide cops. No humor at all.

Just seven sets of eyes on me—the link between three brutal slayings that were so close to one another, it seemed not the work of a serial killer but of a mass murderer.

"Please describe your last conversation with Nate Gundersen," Boyle said.

"He showed up at an Indian restaurant, where I was."

"Were you there alone?"

I stared at Krull. "I was with John."

Boyle said, "Johnny, could you leave the room? I think what we'll do is question you separately."

The minute Krull exited, I felt a loosening in my chest. And only then did I realize how nervous his presence had made me when it came to talking about Nate—especially Nate last night. "Nate showed up at the restaurant, uninvited."

"Was John friendly with him?"

"Are you kidding? He hated him." *Should I have said that?*

Pierce said, "Is it true that Jenna Sargent told him you and the victim were having an affair?"

"Yes . . . Wait a minute, how do you know about that?"

Boyle said, "Let's keep the questioning of the officers for outside the interview room."

Does Pierce know that Krull ran a DNA test on those hairs? Does everyone?

"Go on, Samantha. In your opinion, was Nate cordial to John when he saw him?"

I exhaled. "He said he needed to talk to me alone, and he promised he'd bring me back in one piece."

Patton said, "And John let you go."

"Right. Anyway, Nate told me that he . . ." *It doesn't matter now. He's gone.* "He . . . had sex with Marla Soble—"

Pierce said, "What?"

"He went to Marla's apartment by chance. And they . . . Well, you've got to know Nate to understand. They talked about Greek tragedy for a few minutes, and then they fell into bed. He says he never even found out her last name."

"What was the date on this?" said Pierce.

"I don't know. He said last week."

"I'm gonna go look at the journal," said Munro, and left the room.

"Anyway, I said he had to tell the police."

"Good girl," said Pierce.

"He asked me for twenty-four hours, just so he could tell his fiancée, and get ready for the . . .

you know . . . the fallout. I agreed. So I went back in the restaurant and fed John this awful lie about Nate wanting a *Shakespearean Idol* audition."

"How did Johnny react?"

"He wasn't buying it."

"Did he get mad?"

I could feel movement, detectives leaning in closer, waiting to hear my answer. *Do they actually think he could have done this?* "Of course he got mad."

"Did he stay with you, or were you separated at all?" said Patton.

"Yes."

"Yes, what?"

"Yes—why do you care so much about where John was? Why are you treating him like a suspect?"

Boyle said, "Sam—"

"I know. Don't question officers, but come on."

"We're looking into anyone who had a motive," said Patton gently. "John had a motive, but—"

"John's not a murderer!" I said it more to myself than to her.

"I know that, Sam," she said. "That's exactly what I was going to say. But listen, the guy was found dead in your art-supplies closet. It obviously wasn't a suicide. I'm just trying to rule out the jealous boyfriend."

I heard myself say, "You can't."

"I can't?"

"Not based on what I can tell you about where he was last night. He disappeared. I have no idea where he went."

Boyle said, "What do you say we switch places, Sam. Hang out in the squad room for a little bit. And we'll get Johnny back in for some private questioning."

Fiona stepped out, and returned moments later with Krull. Neither he, nor any of the other detectives, looked at me as I left the interview room.

Whatever Krull's alibi was, it didn't take very long to talk about. I'd been sitting in one of the visitor's chairs for ten minutes at the most when I was called back into the interview room. Krull was staring at the floor. Everyone else was listening to Boyle saying something about "following up on those leads"—and looking glum as he said it—but as soon as he noticed me opening the door, he shut up fast.

I sensed a strange new tension in the air— directed at Krull, or me. Maybe both of us.

Why wouldn't any of these cops look me in the eye?

Fortunately it didn't last. Munro knocked on the door, and entered with a thick, leather-bound book. "Ah, yes, the journal," said Pierce, and everyone snapped back to normal.

"So in case any of you were wondering," Munro said, "Nate Gundersen wasn't the father of Marla's child."

I said, "Excuse me?"

"Here's an entry from about a week ago." Munro read: " 'Made love to a beautiful actor I've seen on TV. I'll never see him again, I'm sure. But it was like living a dream—and being pregnant enhanced the experience.' "

My eyes widened.

"I told you she was cheating," said Pierce.

Boyle said, "With Lucas, of all people!"

"But it was just a onetime thing," I said. "She was a fan."

"It wasn't just with Gundersen," Pierce said. "She was jerkin' Gil's chain as long as she knew him."

Boyle said, "She was two months pregnant. And Professor Valdez knew it. We're not releasing that to the press out of respect for her family. But it sure as shit makes him a person of interest."

"How do you know it wasn't his baby?"

"He had a vasectomy," said Patton. "But he was going to marry her anyway." She rubbed her eyes, then gazed up at the ceiling. "He thought the baby should have a father."

"Why is that relevant?" said Krull.

"Huh?"

"Are you trying to say he's no longer a person of interest because he thought the baby should have a father?"

"Of course not," said Patton. "I was one of the people who thought we should question Valdez in the first place. I'm just saying—"

"He said he'd stick around and help change diapers, so therefore he'd never kill anyone? He's a fucking angel of a dad. Jesus, you sound just like Sam."

I stared at him.

"Take it easy, John," said Boyle. "It's been a tough day, and I think we should all step back."

Krull's eyes were hard as flint. "My mom died when I was a kid, and my dad didn't go anywhere. He stuck around and raised my brother and me, and you know what, Sam? He was a hard-assed, withholding piece of shit, and I wished, every day, that he'd fucking do us a favor and leave."

Pierce said, "You know we're getting this all on tape."

Krull yanked the tape recorder out of the wall and threw it across the room, narrowly missing Boyle's head.

For a dragging moment, the only sound in the world was that of metal and plastic bashing into the wall, then breaking apart as it hit the floor.

Everything's fixable, I wanted to say, to ease the

tension. To stop this awful, vibrating silence. But I couldn't get my mouth to open.

Had the tape recorder landed inches to the left, it would've crushed his partner's skull.

"Sorry." Krull looked at Boyle, then at me.

All I could do was watch him—like Boyle, like everyone else in the room sat watching Krull, until finally he got up and left, closing the door softly behind him.

Minutes later, the spell lifted a little, and we all started filing out of the interview room. "Guess we need a new tape recorder," said Boyle.

Nobody replied; nobody even smiled.

I saw Krull sitting at his desk, his head in his hands, and thought, *It's just been a long day. He's tired. He's emotional. But he's not violent. He's not.*

I was considering walking over to him, asking what had happened, when Patton pulled me into the stairwell. "You okay?" she said.

I looked at her. "That supposed to be a trick question?"

"No, Sam, I—"

"Because . . . from what I can tell, three people were murdered because of me, one of whom I used to love more than, I don't know. Breathing. And . . . and . . . I'm having a few problems with my current relationship, in case you haven't noticed."

Patton put both hands on my shoulders, looking into my eyes. "Krull didn't kill those people," she said softly.

"I know that," I said. "But . . . how do you know? Did he give you an alibi?"

She hugged me, and I felt a twinge of hope, the way I had when Pierce had told me Krull hadn't lied about the press conference. "Are you just trying to make me feel better?" I asked.

"He's my partner. I know him. I know what he's capable of. He didn't do it."

Why didn't she answer my question about the alibi? And why does she sound like she's praying too?

I heard myself say, "Would you have thought he was capable of throwing that tape recorder at Boyle?"

"Listen," she said. "If John had really been throwing it at Art, he wouldn't have missed."

Should I press her about the alibi—or leave it alone? Whatever Krull had said alone with the detectives in the interview room, she obviously thought it was best I didn't hear about it.

"Isn't it always important to know the truth?" I'd asked Sydney last night.

And she'd replied, *"No."*

Before Patton left the stairwell to join her partners in the squad room, I borrowed her cell phone and tapped in Sydney's number.

I expected her voice mail again, and when I got

her actual voice instead, I wasn't sure what to say to it.

"Mom. I . . . hear you're in New York." That seemed as good a place to start as any.

"Yes, Samantha. The Big Apple."

"Why didn't you call me? Why haven't I seen you?"

"I wanted to get settled in first, honey. You know, unpack my things, learn my way around. That way, we could be on equal footing, and you wouldn't be stuck with some needy old sympathy vulture."

"That's ridiculous. I'm your daughter."

"By the way, Vito and I had another falling-out. He wanted me auburn, but I said, 'Better dead than red.'" She laughed heartily. "Samantha? Are you there?"

I gritted my teeth. *She must know what happened to Nate at least. It has to be all over the local radio.* "I'm very hurt you haven't tried to get hold of me today."

"Why today?"

"Are you not in New York City? Do you live in a cave or something?"

She took a long pause. "I could do without the sarcasm."

"But—"

Click. She hung up on me. And I thought, *How could she be so warm to me when she has no idea who I am, and so cold to me when she does?*

When I walked into the squad room, Krull was at his desk, filling out paperwork, his two partners talking in the open area behind him. I watched Krull until he finally glanced up, and we held each other's gaze for several seconds. I didn't feel the need to move any closer, didn't feel the need to ask him questions or talk at all.

For one brief moment, his face from the interview room flashed in my mind—the hardness in his eyes, the twist of rage around his mouth, just before he threw the tape recorder. What had anyone done to make him act that way? What was it that he'd said to Patton? *"You sound just like Sam."*

He got up and joined his partners. But before he did, he nodded at me—as if he'd made some sort of decision.

Having left Ezra with his nanny, Soccoro, Jenna showed up at the precinct house with that awful collage.

The collage was admitted as evidence, and Jenna was questioned for around fifteen minutes. I took her to the break room afterward and bought her an orange soda from one of the vending machines, and we sat at the long table in front of a muted, wall-mounted TV turned to CNN.

"Your boyfriend is very nice," she said. "All the detectives are."

I took a sip of my orange soda. There was

something comforting about the cold can, the bubbles, the vaguely pharmaceutical tang. Orange soda always tasted the way you expected it to taste—no surprises.

"I'm so sorry, Jenna."

"I can't believe he was put in Ezra's classroom. I mean . . . what kind of psycho would—"

"A psycho who had keys to my art-supplies closet," I said, more to myself than to her.

Jenna said, "Do they have any idea who did it?"

"They have some leads," I said. I swallowed hard. My face felt numb. *He didn't do it. He didn't do it. He didn't do it.*

Jenna was saying, "Why would anybody want to kill Nate? He could be really infuriating. But . . . he was so much fun."

"What did the cops ask you about?"

"Oh, his sex problem, our fights . . . the usual. This probably sounds weird, but I kind of *liked* being jealous of every person he ever hung out with. It made me appreciate what I had."

"You know what, Jenna?"

"What?"

"You really were the perfect woman for him."

"Yeah, well . . . Hey, would you look at that? Nate made the crawl."

I turned toward the TV and saw the news of Nate's death scrolling across the bottom of the screen, under the face of a smiling female anchor who was obviously discussing something different—sports scores, perhaps, or fall fashions. SOAP STAR STABBED TO DEATH, it said. Not much more than that, other than Nate's name, and the fact that he was twenty-nine years old.

"He always wanted to be on that damn CNN crawl," Jenna said. Then she put her head down on the table, and finally, she started to cry.

Jenna had taken her own car to the precinct house, parking it just up the street, so I told the detectives I'd be back in a minute, and walked her to her car.

Word had apparently spread about Nate's murder, because outside the door of the precinct house, reporters and photographers and, most of all, fans had suddenly cropped up like dandelions.

"Jenna!" the photographers shouted. "Look over here, please, Jenna! We're very sorry for your loss."

"Oh, my God, it's Blythe!"

"Who's that she's with?"

"Nobody."

Some of the fans were thrill seekers, interested in nothing more than the next high-profile murder mystery; some were pasty-faced ghouls like the Marlamaniacs. But some seemed to genuinely grieve.

There was one young girl dressed all in black who'd Scotch-taped Nate's *Soap Opera Digest* cover to the front of her black T-shirt. She reminded me of Tabitha, only she was easily six years younger. An actual child.

I caught the girl's eye, and she spoke. She didn't raise her voice enough for me to hear her over all the talking and the traffic sounds, but I could read her lips: *Did you love him too?*

I nodded.

Finally, I was able to pry Jenna away from everyone, down the stairs, and to her Volvo up the street. "You know how I first got Nate into bed?" she said, before she got in. "I told him that Lucas reminded me of Jim, the gentleman caller from *Glass Menagerie*."

"His favorite role."

"Then I took my shirt off."

"That'll do it."

She gave me a huge, warm smile. "You know, if I didn't have Ezra to take care of, I'd kill myself tonight."

Before I could think of how to respond, she got in her car and drove off.

Without a soap star in tow, it took minimal effort to get past the phalanx of fans and through the heavy glass doors of the precinct house. Climbing the stairs, I started to frame the conversation I planned to have with Krull that night. *John, we need to talk.* No, he hated that. *John, can we discuss a couple of matters?* Better.

What was I doing, though? Did he rehearse that outburst in the interview room? Did he worry about my feelings, think about what I hated to see and hear and discover before he . . . *He didn't do it. He didn't do it. He didn't do it.*

When I walked into the squad room, the only detectives around were Boyle and Patton.

"Where's John?" I asked them.

They looked at each other.

"What?"

Boyle said, "It's just a technicality. Everybody knows that Johnny's as good a good guy as they come. The only reason why they're doing it is to rule him out."

"So you're trying to tell me that—"

"John's a person of interest," Patton said "Very minor interest."

No . . .

"Just trying to get all their ducks in a row," said Boyle.

"But they're *your* ducks. It's your case!"

He seemed to force his face into a smile. "Detectives from the Tenth are questioning him. We're too close."

"So . . ." I said. "The Tenth thinks he's a person of interest. That's Marla's precinct. They're probably focusing on that one, not Nate." I looked at Patton. "They're not just ruling out the jealous boyfriend."

"John Krull is not a murderer," said Boyle.

"What alibi did he give you guys?"

"You really need to ask him that yourself," Patton said.

"He didn't have one, did he?"

"Sam, listen to yourself," said Boyle. "This is John. He'd lay down his life for you."

"What would you do if you found out something about me? Something that . . . isn't good."

"John and I," I said quietly, "we just . . . need to talk."

"It's been a rough day," said Patton. "We're all a little unhinged."

Boyle nodded. "Mercury's in retrograde; whole world's fucked up."

"Is that where he is now? At the Tenth?"

Patton said she was pretty sure he was waiting for the squad car, but out back to avoid the crowd.

I hurried outside, down the alleyway next to the precinct house, and into the back parking lot, where I saw Krull leaning against the wall, smoking a cigarette. "Hi," he said.

"What happened to your hands?"

"I told you—"

"Don't say bar fight to me again, John. You

don't get in bar fights. Where were you all night last night? Where were you the night before? Don't say walking, John. Nobody goes walking for four hours in a thunderstorm. I want straight answers."

"Sam," he said, quietly, "can you save the questions for after I finish getting questioned? Please?"

I looked at those sad black eyes, the gentle mouth, the nose I knew he'd broken as a kid while jumping off his roof, pretending to be Superman. It was the kindest face I'd ever known.

"Sam, you don't think I killed those people, do you?"

"Of course not." I put both arms around John Krull, held him as close as I could.

The squad car pulled up, turning into the alley. He got into the backseat, and I slid in beside him. We hadn't discussed this; some things just went without saying.

Of course the Tenth Precinct detectives wouldn't let me join Krull in the interview room, so I went back to their break area, which had vending machines, a long table and a wall-mounted TV, turned off. I bought myself another orange soda, found the power button and turned to CNN. The main story seemed to be about the September 11 anniversary, which would take place in exactly a week, but Nate's murder had taken over the crawl.

SLAIN SOAP OPERA STAR NATE GUNDERSEN WAS "A TRUE HUMANITARIAN," SAYS NEW YORK MAYOR MICHAEL BLOOMBERG.

MEANWHILE, THE SEARCH CONTINUES FOR GUNDER-SEN'S KILLER. . . .

What a strange feeling it was to see his name skittering across the national news like that, under footage of the burning Trade Center. No link was described between Nate and the two other murders. Nikolas did make the crawl too, but as a completely different story: (A YOUNG MAN WAS FOUND DEAD IN AN OFF-OFF-BROADWAY THEATER. POSSIBLY DRUG RELATED.) The cops hadn't given out the information connecting the slayings, and, being the source of that information, I was grateful.

Across from where I was sitting, through a long rectangular window, the setting sun glowed pinkish lavender, and I felt a feeble relief; at least this day was over.

New York sunsets look like drugstore eye shadow. I put my head down on the table and closed my eyes.

"Fancy seeing you here . . . and I do mean *fancy.*"

I looked up and saw Marla sitting across the table. She wore a bright red sequined cocktail dress and matching lipstick.

"What are you doing in my precinct?"

"I'm waiting for John."

"Is he still in that silly interrogation? I hate to think I went and got him arrested—and all just because of the show."

"The show?"

"You know. With the knife, and the blood . . . It's a new finale we're working up for *Shakespearean Idol.* Nate and I are playing Corky and Juliana. We've got awesome chemistry."

"So you're alive?"

She tossed her shiny brown hair over her shoulders. "Don't I look it?"

"That's such great news. We have to tell *everybody.* We have to tell the police!"

Abruptly, she leaned in so close, her mouth nearly touched mine. "First, could I ask your honest opinion about something?"

"Okay."

"Can you see my autopsy scars? I tried putting makeup over them, but they just keep showing. Especially from where they took my brain out."

I jolted awake to see Krull sitting across the table from me, in the exact same seat where Marla had sat in my dream.

"You were snoring," he said.

"That's embarrassing."

I watched him for a few moments. "So. How did it go?" I said. But I needn't have. You could tell how it went by the paleness of his face, the tightness of his jaw.

Krull said, "Ever hear of Capgras Syndrome?"

"Is it a disease?"

"Sort of . . . It's more like a neurological disorder. Pierce was telling me about it the other day at the gym."

"What is it?"

"It's where you wake up one morning, and you think everyone close to you—your girlfriend, your parents, your friends, even your pets—you think they're all exact doubles, masquerading."

"If you think they're all *exact* doubles, how are you supposed to prove that wrong?"

"You can't really. In fact, a lot of people who have it go on for years, relating to their wife, their friends, their pets as if they're the same people, the same animals. But in their hearts, they're terrified."

"Well," I said, "no matter how bad things get, you can say, 'At least I don't have Capgras Syndrome.'"

"That's not why I brought it up."

"Well, what, then? You think you have it? Do you feel like I'm a replica?"

"No," he said. "I feel like *I'm* the replica. I feel like . . . I was one guy when you met me. But inside me, there's always been this whole other guy and he's . . . consumed the guy you know. From within."

I looked at him. "You're freaking me out, John."

"I'm sorry. There's just . . . There's so much I want to show you. But I'm afraid."

"Why?"

"I'm afraid you're not going to like what you see. And . . . that's going to kill me, because even though you've never seen it before, it's who I am."

His gaze darted around the precinct break room; then he looked so deep into my face it startled me. "Do you understand what I'm trying to tell you? I can't say it in here."

Suddenly, my spine felt as if it were coated in thick ice. I couldn't move, could hardly breathe. *He didn't do it. He didn't do it. He didn't . . .*

Krull's cell phone rang. He flipped it open and looked at the screen.

"Who is calling you?"

"I gotta go," he said.

"You're not going anywhere until you explain what the hell you mean."

He kissed me on the forehead. "You know what? Forget I ever said anything," he said. "That was just this terrible day talking."

"Unless I heard wrong, you're trying to tell me about a secret life?"

"I really gotta go."

"Can you just answer one question for me, please?" I said slowly. "You don't have to answer anything else—and you can leave right away. I just want you to be truthful."

He shifted his head from side to side, as if he were literally weighing the concept in his mind. "Okay."

"In your secret life—the life I don't know about. Did someone . . ." I closed my eyes, opened them again. "Were you struggling with someone who bit your hands?"

His gaze was steady, almost laserlike. "Yes."

My breath grew shallow. "Thanks."

"I'll see you later." And with that, he ran off into the darkness that pressed against the building.

12

The Quiet Invisible

I stood in the break room, staring at the CNN crawl until the news stories started repeating themselves. Then I ran outside and to the street corner, where I grabbed a cab that seemed to pull up out of nowhere.

"Where did you just come from?" I asked the driver.

"Heaven."

I peered into the rearview mirror at a pinched, bearded face.

"Store opening uptown. Heaven. Lots of rich people there."

The radio was tuned to WLUV. "We'll be right back with Dr. Sydney's 'Art of Caring,'" the announcer said.

I looked at my watch. Seven thirty."I thought she wasn't on until eight."

"It's a rebroadcast," he said.

My mother's voice floated out of the car radio. "Welcome back to Dr. Sydney's 'Art of Caring.' I care about you. Next up, we have Sarah from Manhattan. Sarah, what can I—"

"Change the station please," I said.

"Okay, okay," said the driver. "I thought everybody loved Dr. Sydney."

"She's not a doctor."

The driver found a baseball game, and I closed my eyes, listening to the soothing monotone of the announcer. I remembered joking around with Krull and Pierce in front of the Yankees game, and realized it had only been yesterday.

It seemed like something out of an old home movie. Even Pierce and Krull's spat had a quaintness to it, a warmth.

When did everything become so strange, so cold?

As soon as we were a few blocks away from the apartment, I asked the driver to stop, and paid him. I wanted to walk the rest of the way. I needed the air, didn't want to go inside. It hit me that no one was watching me right now. I knew it for a fact, because Krull wasn't around.

As I passed a busy playground, I recalled a time, over the summer, when Krull and I had walked by the same place. For quite a while we watched this one little boy pushing his baby brother on a swing. Back and forth, back and forth, he did it with infinite gentleness and patience, making the little boy squeal and laugh incessantly. I grinned at Krull, expecting a comment on how cute they were, what good brothers, but was shocked by the pall over his face. "That's as happy as they'll ever be," he said. "Before everything starts to hurt."

Maybe there was another reason for Krull's disappearances, for the Sterling roses on the bodies, for the fear in Nikolas's eyes when Krull had approached him in Starbucks, for all those notes, warning me not to make "him" angry. Maybe there was another reason why he'd run out into a rainstorm after I'd said, "We shouldn't have moved in together"—the same night a woman was killed, then removed, from my old apartment.

But what other reason could there be for the bite marks on his hands? His violent behavior in the interview room? The "secret life" he'd started to describe?

I grabbed hold of the playground gate and squeezed my eyes against a rush of tears. *"I love you so much,"* I said, doubling over with a pain so great—the pain of my heart breaking.

My lover was not a superhero. He was a monster. And everything hurt.

*   *   *

When I got to Stuyvesant Town, I bypassed my building in favor of Pierce's, then took the elevator up to his haunted eighth-floor apartment and rang the doorbell. I was aware of his eye watching me through the peephole, and then his voice, "Sam!" before the door opened. He was wearing a Yankees T-shirt and shorts, holding a bowl of Froot Loops.

I smiled, making my voice as casual as possible. "Hey, Zachary! How's the ghost?"

"Pain in the ass. He keeps turning my radio to this opera station. Can I get you something? Cereal?"

"Actually, I wanted to ask you a huge favor."

When I left Pierce's apartment, my purse, chock-full as it was already, felt five times heavier thanks to the unloaded semiautomatic I was now carrying. It had been easy enough to explain the need to Pierce.

I had a stalker after all. And Krull wasn't always around to protect me. It did feel a bit odd having this serious conversation in Pierce's disgusting bachelor pad, with its dirty pink shag rug, beer-stained pullout couch and *Playboy* centerfolds from the mid-nineties taped to the walls. But Pierce didn't seem to notice. He asked which of his three guns I'd like, made sure I knew how to hold it properly, clicked open the magazine to assure me it wasn't loaded.

Just before I left, Pierce had said, "Doesn't John have a service revolver?"

"Yeah . . . but he keeps it in a safe. And I don't know the combination."

He smiled. "Try your birthday, or the anniversary of your first date. That's what I would use if I were him—something connected with you."

"That's sweet, Zachary."

"I'm a sweet guy. You sure you don't want any Froot Loops?"

Krull wasn't home yet when I arrived. I didn't expect him to be. Though I had no idea how far away he'd gone after receiving that cell phone call, something told me he'd be there for a while.

I didn't even bother turning on the lights in the living room. After I was through pouring Jake's dinner into a bowl, I sat on the couch in the gentle darkness, listening to the cat smacking his lips and then, when that finally subsided, to what Nate used to call "the quiet invisible."

"Turn off the TV and sit next to me, Samantha. Listen to the beautiful quiet invisible."

I looked at my watch. Eight o'clock. The couple next door wouldn't start up anytime soon.

Poor Nate. You have nothing but quiet invisible now.

Riing.

I answered the phone to a soft female voice that sounded exactly like my mother's. "Samantha?"

"Ummm . . . yes?"

"How are you feeling?"

"Well, I'm not bored, that's for sure." I glanced at the caller ID screen (PRIVATE NUMBER), then let my eyes drift to the message counter on the answering machine, saw a flashing F for full.

"This must be such a difficult time for you," the voice was saying. "I'm so sorry."

Was Sydney actually apologizing for hanging up on me today? "Mom?"

"So did he kill him?"

"Excuse me?"

"A highly placed police source tells us John Krull is a person of interest in the Nate Gundersen murder."

"Who is this?"

"Anne Rogers with the *Daily News*."

I hung up the phone.

I checked the messages. There was one from Yale. ("I saw it on CNN, honey. Can we please just make this stop?") And yes, one from my mother. ("Samantha, dear, I'm terribly sorry for your loss. Listen to my show tonight—I'll be paying tribute to your Nate. He was such a nice boy.") But sure enough, all the rest were interview requests—the *Post*, the *Times*, *Newsday*, *NY1 Cable*, local news from all four networks . . .

even *Soap Opera Digest*. I looked at Jake. "Somebody blabbed." Probably those cops from the Tenth.

We kept our stereo in a cabinet under the TV. It was switched to the CD player, so when I turned it on, I was nearly knocked over by the AC/DC CD that Krull had, at some point, been listening to at eardrum-shattering volume. "We're on the highway to hell," screamed the singer.

You can say that again, Angus, or whatever your name is.

I turned down the volume and switched over to the radio. WLUV wasn't hard to find—it was on the right side of the AM dial, one of the strongest stations in the city.

I recognized my mother's voice immediately. It sounded even smoother, even gentler than it had on the phone. And what she was saying was, "... Love him."

A few, dramatic seconds of dead air. Then, "That's what Samantha said. 'I love him, Mom.' What could I tell her? What can you tell a headstrong, twenty-one-year-old girl? Even if you know she's about to make the biggest mistake of her whole, fool life."

My heart thumped against my ribs. *This is Sydney's tribute?* I shut off the radio, but half a second later, I switched it back on.

"... was it a mistake? Was it really?"

I dropped to the floor and sat down, cross-legged, like a child. Then I lay on my back, closed my eyes as if she were telling me a bedtime story.

"I met him once," Sydney said. "At a party, after their college graduation. He didn't say much. Boys that age tend to be quiet with their elders. But I do recall one exchange we had. 'Nathan,' I said to him. 'If you want to become an actor, why are you driving all the way to New York? Why don't you two just get an apartment in L.A.? That's where all the movies are.' Do you know what he said?"

Another stretch of dead air.

"He said, 'Mrs. Stark-Leiffer, I like waiting in the wings. That moment just before going on-stage is so exciting. It's my favorite thing about acting. Movies,' he said, 'Movies don't have wings.'

"My daughter drove all the way across the country with a boy, moved to a city where she didn't know anyone, a city with—I'm sorry—lousy weather . . . just so he could have his wings. Not so he could make money and support her. The theater doesn't pay well, and he didn't even think about soap operas until after they broke up. Not so she could ride on his coattails to fame. Fame—in some god-awful off-off-Broadway experiment? In some ridiculous Disney musical, getting drowned out by the sound of babies crying in the audience? Please! My daughter sacrificed her life so he could have his wings, listeners! That's love.

"No matter where you think Nate Gundersen has gone, whether it's heaven, or nirvana, or maybe another life to start all over again, he goes there having inspired a feeling that strong—that selfless—in another human being. He goes there with wings. I'll be taking calls after the break."

When I opened my eyes, a couple of pent-up tears streamed down my face. "Thanks, Mom," I whispered.

Next to me on the floor was Pierce's semiautomatic. Throughout the night, I'd keep it close enough to grab. I picked it up and, for a long time, I just lay there, feeling the cool weight of it in my hands.

After listening to about five home-loan commercials in a row, I turned off the radio, crept over to our bedroom and cracked the door.

"Goddamn you!"

I jumped back, but recovered fast. I knew it was just our neighbor, yelling at his churchin' wife.

"Bet she never waited up for you, holding a semiautomatic," I said.

Based only on what I was capable of doing, I'd formed a rough plan in my head: When Krull came home, I would hold the gun on him, force him to give me all the details of his secret life. And if what he said matched what I feared, we'd find him a good lawyer and call Boyle or Patton together.

I was not capable of shooting Krull, which was why the gun wasn't loaded. And I wasn't capable of leaving him—not without hearing the truth first.

"You can't leave me!" the woman next door shrieked. "I'm already gone!"

I opened the closet door, stared down at Krull's safe. What did he keep in there? Why didn't I know the combination?

"Try your birthday, or the anniversary of your first date."

Our first real date had been in early March 2001. Krull had just gotten out of the hospital, and he still wore a bandage over the bullet wound in his neck. I took a personal day from my job at the Space. We had a few beers at a Mexican place on Fourteenth Street, then took the nine train down to Battery Park and watched the lavender-pink sunset from the observatory at the World Trade Center. "I've always loved it up here," Krull said. "You look down, and there's no drama. Just lights and rooftops and traffic. Everything moves at just the right speed."

I turned the combination. Left one. Right seven. Left seventy-three. *He used my birthday.* I let myself feel flattered for just a few seconds. Then I opened the door.

First I saw his service revolver, but when I lifted it out, I noticed rows and rows of white business envelopes, then a few piles of glossy rectangles. Photographs. Turned over.

In my mind flashed the killer's "All About Me" collage—that twisted gift in Nate's dressing room. *He takes pictures, stores them in that safe.*

"Oh, God."

I picked one up and held it in my hands. But I couldn't bring myself to look at it.

I held my breath, closed my eyes, counted to seven.

"I don't know what good you think luck will do," said Krull. The only person in the world who ever noticed my superstitions anymore. In the room with me. I hadn't heard him come in. But that was nothing new. I never heard him come in.

"You opened my safe," he said.

"I had to."

"I didn't want you to find out like this."

I whirled around, and showed him Pierce's semi. "Don't come near me," I said.

"Jesus, Sam, where did you get—"

"I mean it."

Krull backed up one step at a time, 'til he was standing halfway across the room.

Only then did I turn the photograph over.

It was a school picture of a smiling little boy in a striped T-shirt against a pale blue background. He had curly hair and large black eyes, and for a few moments I just stood there, a panicky confusion washing through me. I looked at Krull's face. "Who is this?"

"That's Ethan," he said carefully. "He's my son."

I didn't feel I had much use for the gun anymore as Krull plucked more items from the safe and spread them out on the bed for me to see. Birthday cards, drawings, little notes that said, *I love you, Daddy,* all from Ethan Brody, Krull's seven-year-old secret son—a sweet kid, but borderline autistic. He had a tendency to scratch and bite and sometimes hit—hence the wounds on Krull's hands, hence his asking me if boys were prone to violence.

Krull had married Ethan's mother, Sheila, when she got pregnant (just like Marla and Gil had been planning to do), but they couldn't make it work. They were divorced, and she took the baby and left town a week after his first birthday.

Krull—who had run DNA tests on my hair—used police software to track down his family in Salt Lake City, Utah. He sent weekly checks, letters . . . all were returned. Until finally Sheila started cashing the checks.

Now, though, she was practically a neighbor.

Sheila and Ethan Brody moved from Salt Lake City to Brooklyn nine months after September 11, when Sheila had reached an "emotional breakthrough" and decided to "stop being such a sympathy vulture" and reunite her son with his father. All this information came from the letters Krull had removed from the safe—this shrine to his secret family.

And, as we looked through it all, I felt such overwhelming mixed emotions that I wanted to cry, just cry and never stop. "Why didn't you tell me, John?" I said.

"Patton wanted me to tell you."

"Patton knew?"

"This afternoon she knew. I told all of them in the interview room. I had to. It was my alibi."

"Your—"

"It's where I've been disappearing to, Sam. I get phone calls from Sheila. Ethan gets out of control, and she needs me to talk him down. Last night . . ." he said. "Last night he punched Sheila in the stomach. I had to restrain him. He bit me. After he finally fell asleep, she was so upset she asked me to sleep on her couch."

"God, John. Why did you keep all this to yourself? I could've helped you. I would've wanted to—"

"I didn't tell you at the beginning because Sheila and Ethan were across the country. All I did was send money. And . . . I know how you feel about dads who leave their families."

"But they left you. You didn't—"

"I could have tried harder to keep them around. I was working up at the Thirty-third, and hardly ever home, and when I was, all I could think about was trying to make detective. I drove them away. And look what happened to him."

"That's not your fault."

"How do you know? I could sit and talk nature/nurture with you to the end of time and neither one of us would—"

I looked at him. "What about when they moved here? Why didn't you tell me then?"

"I was . . . afraid . . . of how you might react."

"Did you honestly think I'd leave you because you have a son?"

"I didn't know."

I picked up one of Ethan's drawings: a smiling head on two stick legs, wearing a policeman's hat. Underneath, in huge, crooked letters, was one word: *Daddy.* "That's what's wrong with us, John. We don't really know each other."

"I know your favorite movie," he said. "Your favorite flower, your favorite baseball team." His face was very serious.

"Yes."

"I know you sometimes snore, and you cry during old episodes of *thirtysomething* and you're

terrified of clowns and I love you more than anyone I've ever met."

A slow warmth filled my chest and a smile
curled my lips, even though I didn't want to
smile. I couldn't help it.

"I also know you have a semiautomatic, and
you apparently aren't afraid to use it."

I sighed. "It's not loaded. . . . I borrowed the
semi from Pierce because I was afraid of . . . what
was in your safe. I thought you had problems.
But it's not you. It's us. *We* have problems."

"I guess we do . . . but—"

"But." I put a hand to his mouth. "Everything's
fixable."

"I'd like to try, Sam. I really would."

"Then let's try."

Krull kissed me with the relief of someone
freed of secrets. "Is it too late to go back to that Indian place?" he said.

I said, "Why the hell not? It's still open." And
as he went into the bathroom to wash up, I whispered, "Take two."

When I picked up the letters and brought them
back to the open safe, I noticed so many more inside. *How could he look at this every morning? I was
sleeping right behind him, sometimes even talking to
him while he was sitting here, his other life right in
front of his eyes.* There were stacks of letters, cards
in childish script with Utah postmarks. And so

many more, with older dates on the postmarks, addressed to Ethan from Krull and marked RE-TURN TO SENDER.

I saw an old pacifier, a stuffed Clifford toy, and wondered, *Did my dad keep mementos of me?*

Yeah, right. My mother ghostwrote his birthday cards.

As I picked up the bright red Clifford dog, I spotted something shiny underneath it. A state-of-the-art silver digital camera. It didn't look like something Krull would own. But then again, until fifteen minutes ago, none of this stuff looked like anything Krull would own.

"By the way!" he shouted from the bathroom. "How did you figure out the combination of my safe?"

"Pierce suggested I try my birthday! He said that's what he would use if it were his safe!"

"Man, that guy has a crush on you."

I turned the camera over, looked at the small stored-pictures screen and pushed the button.

Krull said, "But he was right!"

The first picture was of a valentine heart, drawn in blood, on an exposed brick wall.

"I chose your birthday because I knew I'd always remember it!"

The next was of a woman's bare leg against some kind of dull pink background, gashed all the way down to the exposed bone.

"Isn't that nice of me?"

After that was a man's chiseled abdomen, a chunk of flesh removed around the belly button. *Nate.*

"Sam?"

What would you do if you found out something about me? Something that . . . isn't good?

"Are you okay, honey?"

I dropped the camera to the floor. "Some things aren't fixable," I whispered.

13

Pillow Talk

I swiped Pierce's semiautomatic off the floor, shoved it in my purse, backed out of the door and bolted down the hall to the elevator. No one had taken it since Krull had come home, so when I hit the button, the doors opened immediately. At least something was going my way tonight.

"Sam! Wait!"

I could hear his footsteps heading down the hall as the door closed and the elevator went down. The one elevator on our entire wing.

Don't celebrate. He'll take the stairs. And he'll be fast about it.

I touched my bag, where I'd put the gun, and stared at the blinking lights announcing each floor as we passed. *Ten, nine, eight . . . keep going. . . .*

The elevator stopped on five. "Shit." I was about to hit the CLOSE DOOR button when a very old woman yelled, "Wait a minute."

"I'm in a huge hurry," I said, between my teeth.

She rammed her foot between the closing doors. "You ever hear of karma, young lady?"

"Yes."

"Kindness and positive energy come back to us tenfold," she said. "So does rudeness." She hit the fourth floor.

"You don't understand. Somebody wants to kill me."

"I don't blame him." When the doors opened again, seconds later, she placed her hand in front of the electric eye. "Hmmm," she said. "Is this really the floor I wanted?"

I removed the gun from my purse. "I'd say it is."

She got out fast.

The elevator reached the lobby and I raced through it. Just a little bit farther. I pushed through the front door, ran through the courtyard onto the street. Three cabs came roaring by, all of them off duty.

He's going to catch up.

I whirled around, tore across the courtyard into Pierce's building and headed through the lobby to the elevator. I hit the button and waited for it to show. Krull was downstairs by now. He had to be. *Don't think of Pierce's place, please don't, please don't.* I crossed my fingers behind my back; then I crossed my wrists, my ankles.

Like a much-anticipated date, the elevator arrived. I hit the eighth floor, ran to Pierce's apartment, banged on the door.

And when he opened it, I saw he was on the phone, saying, "I'm still enjoying that twelve-pack."

My eyes wide, I mouthed the word *no.*

"Sam?" He looked at me, forehead knotted with confusion. "No. Umm . . . no, she's not here, John. Maybe you just misplaced her; she's pretty small." He chuckled. "Okay then. Yeah, I'll let you know if she calls."

After he hung up, I threw my arms around his neck and hugged him. "Thank you, Zachary."

"Uhh . . . I gotta say, I'm a little confused."

"That makes two of us. Invite me in; I'll explain."

Pierce's couch smelled of stale beer, and sitting on the left side, I got an embarrassingly intimate view of 1995's Playmate of the Year. It was not the kind of place I usually found warm and welcoming. But tonight, there was nowhere else I'd rather be.

I glanced at a dark blue sleeping bag, unfurled

in the corner on the dirty shag rug. "I don't sleep there," Pierce said. "The ghost does. I use the couch."

I stared at him.

He gave me a nervous smile. "That was a joke. Ummm . . . you want a beer or something?"

"If you don't mind," I said. "Can I tell you what happened tonight?"

"Yeah, of course," he said, and I proceeded to describe Krull's mood swings, my growing, gnawing suspicion of him. "Oh, Sam," said Pierce. "John wouldn't—"

But then I asked if he'd seen the gruesome "All About Me" collage that Jenna had found in Nate's dressing room. And after he said, "Yes," I told him about the digital camera that Krull kept in his safe—about each picture I'd seen stored in it.

His eyes widened. "My God."

"Who knows how long he's had these urges?" I said. "Who knows how many other people he's killed?"

"Maybe," he said. "But this is . . . it's all about you, isn't it, Sam?"

"Huh?"

"He killed those three people for you—Nate 'cause he thought you were sleeping with him, Nikolas 'cause he wouldn't stop sending you those notes, and Marla 'cause she lived where you used to live."

I sighed.

"Maybe it stops and starts with you—and if he gets help, it'll all be over."

"He slashed them up and took pictures, Zachary. He cut a chunk out of Nate's stomach."

He turned to me, a look of raw fear on his face. "What do you think we should do?"

"Let's go to the precinct house, okay? You have a car?"

"Yeah, yeah. Help me find my keys—they might be in the kitchen drawer."

I hurried into his tiny kitchen. The counter was surprisingly clean, especially compared to the rest of this place. There was more than one drawer, of course. Pierce had never been terribly specific about things.

How strange that I was terrified of Krull, and the only cop who could help me was the most overreactive one in the whole precinct. *They'd better not think Pierce is crying wolf again.* Why hadn't I taken the camera with me?

I slipped open a drawer. There was a set of keys inside, but not one of them looked as if it belonged in an ignition. Behind them was another set, which I pulled out, then another. *He obviously has a key drawer.* But when I looked closer at the set I'd just removed, I felt the tiny hairs stand up on the back of my neck.

One of the keys was a dense, five-inch-long rectangle with piranha teeth. *Another SAF-T brand. What are the odds?*

I reached into my overstuffed bag, produced my apartment keys, my classroom keys, keys to the Space's box office and theater.

They were identical.

I didn't need to pull the last set out. I knew what they were just from looking at them. The keys to Marla's five dead bolts.

He'd made copies of all my keys. And he started doing it last year, when I still lived in that apartment.

An icy dread seeped out of the core of my chest, into my legs, up through my scalp.

I backed up, but connected with Pierce's broad, bulky chest. One of his overstuffed arms slipped around my neck. "I think we should stay home instead," he said softly.

I felt cloth in my face, coated with something that smelled sickly sweet, like bad air freshener. *Wait,* I tried to say. And then everything went black.

What hit me first, as I started to wake up, was the awful throbbing, as if my skull were suddenly too big for the skin that covered it, and the feel of my eyeballs—slippery and dense, like hard-boiled eggs.

My tongue was completely dried out. What I

really wanted was to walk into the kitchen and get myself a huge glass of water, but the thought of getting up made me dizzy. . . . *Man, do I have a hangover.*

I remembered the cheap wine at the Indian restaurant, followed by that exquisite twelve-year-old, which I must have polished off as well. *Why else would I be feeling like this? Why else would I have called my mother's program last night? Did I really do that?*

Then my eyelids started to flutter. I remembered a seemingly endless dream. . . . *Yale calling, and the stranger from Starbucks dead onstage. Jenna Sargent, showing Terry and me that gruesome "All About Me" collage. Then Nate . . . in the art-supplies closet . . . Krull was a father, and then a murderer. . . . Then something about Pierce. Pierce and my keys . . .*

What a horrible dream, I thought. Until I realized I couldn't move my arms or legs. I felt the gaffer's tape around my ankles, and something else fastening my wrists behind my back. Handcuffs. The new, plastic kind used by police officers.

It was not a dream, but I was in bed. I could feel thick pillows under my head, neck, upper back, a cool, soft smoothness under my bare arms and bound hands. A satin comforter.

Not my bed. A bed. I'd never owned a satin comforter in my life.

Slowly, I opened my eyes. My vision was

blurry, so I couldn't discern shapes right away, but I was overwhelmed by one color. Green. Everything was green.

As my eyes started to adjust, I was able to pick out the emerald comforter beneath me, the avocado-colored walls, a sea-foam vase atop a teal dresser. Even the TV—set up across from where I lay propped up on those pillows like a hospital patient—the TV had been painted a flat grass green. All green, except the blue-and-white Dodgers penant on the wall, the Sterling roses in the vase.

I became vaguely aware of a man's voice, humming in my ear, before becoming more distinct. ". . . look so pretty here . . ."

"Pierce?" My voice came out frail and croaky.

His shaved head appeared in front of my face. "Please call me Zachary. I love that."

"Where am—"

"My bedroom. Your bedroom. You like it, right? Green's your favorite. I have all your favorites." He hit a remote control, and dancing munchkins appeared on the TV. "Ding-dong, the witch is dead," they sang.

The Wizard of Oz.

"I . . . didn't know you . . . ?"

"You didn't know I had a bedroom? No one does. It's my secret. Like my hobby." He stared into my face. "Like you."

His eyes were huge and mud-colored, wide with insanity. Why hadn't I noticed that before?

"Ezra said you like polar bears. I saw that polar bear on your 'All About Me' collage, and Ezra said it's because they're your favorite."

"You talked to Ezra?"

"Oh, yeah, we're buddies."

I remembered Ezra, curled up in a ball under my desk.

"What are you doing down here, honey?"

"Hiding from monsters."

"I talked to him and his nanny when they were leaving school yesterday. Anybody will talk to you if you show 'em a badge." He grinned. "And if you get very, very close to them, and tell them you'll cut their pretty mommy if they say a word to anyone . . . they'll keep a secret, too."

"Superheroes save people," I heard myself say. "Monsters take them away."

"What's that supposed to mean?"

"Nothing."

He lay down next to me and I held my breath. "Anyway, Ezra said you like polar bears, which made me know for sure we're soul mates."

From the back pocket of his shorts, he pulled out a long, mean-looking hunting knife and held it in front of my eyes. On its black metal hilt someone had painted a white bear standing on his hind legs, his mouth roared open, revealing sharp black teeth. "I like polar bears too."

I closed my eyes, focused on the munchkins' voices, singing on TV. "She's gone where the goblins go, below, below, below. . . ." I pulled at the handcuffs.

And then I felt warm breath on my face. I opened my eyes and saw Pierce, so close his eyes blurred into one. "I just gotta kiss you," he said.

I bit his lip hard, and he grabbed both my shoulders, pushed me back onto the pillows.

"What the fuck are you doing?" I saw a trickle of blood edging down his chin and felt a dim satisfaction, until he straddled my stomach, putting all his bulky weight on me, so my breath came out in shallow, desperate gasps. He took out the polar-bear knife and touched the tip of the sharp blade to the delicate skin just behind my earlobe. "I bet your blood is beautiful." He wiped his mouth with the back of his hand, the one not holding the knife. "Redder than Marla's. Redder than my mom's." I felt the sting of the blade, a warm trickle edging down my neck. "Mom called me Zachary, too. I cut her throat when she was sleeping."

Help me, help me, I thought, my heart pounding against my ribs. Until slowly, Pierce took the blade away, touched his thick fingers to the skin and stared at them, slick with my blood. "Beautiful."

"We represent the Lollypop Guild, the Lollypop Guild. . . ."

"Please put the knife away." I felt two tears oozing out of the corners of my eyes. *Deep breath. Okay. Stay calm.*

"Don't look at me like that."

"Like what?"

"Like someone who's never stabbed another person to death. You know how it feels. Quit playing like you don't."

"I . . ."

"I know you, Sam. I know you better than anybody." He pressed his bloodied fingers to his lips, and for a second, I could almost hear that sound again, the horrible draining of someone else's life, the death rattle. I hadn't wanted to kill that murderer. I only wanted to call the police. But I couldn't. I had to . . . *The blood, leaking out of the dead body's mouth . . .*

"It feels awful."

He punched the pillow next to my head, and a thin gasp escaped from my throat.

"I did this for you. All of it, and now you're acting like . . . like fucking *Nikolas*. What's wrong with you? You don't whimper. You're a killer."

I gritted my teeth, stared up at this dense-bodied, bald psychopath I'd come to for help. *I'm such a crappy judge of character.*

Should I risk screaming? Stuy Town walls were

thin, as I knew from my fighting neighbors. Someone was bound to hear me and call 911. First, though, I needed him off me. And I needed for him to give me that knife.

How can I get out of this? And like an answer, a familiar sentence popped into my head: *"If you stop acting like a victim, he'll stop treating you like one."* Who said that? Doesn't matter. It's good advice.

I made my voice as steady, as calm as I could. "You know, you're fast with that knife."

Pierce's features softened a little, and for a moment, he seemed to transform back into the cop I knew. The cop who yelled at Yankees games and offered Froot Loops to his visitors.

"It's impressive."

"Thanks," he said. "You gonna be nice to me now?"

"Yes."

He moved off my stomach, touched the tip of the blade to my lips, to my cheeks, to the hollow of my throat. "This place is a big change for you, but I know you're gonna like it," he said. "I know you."

The Wicked Witch of the West said, "Well my little pretty, I can cause accidents too," and for the next few moments, I forgot all about who I really was, forgot what my own voice sounded like. My mother filled my head—the one person I knew who was nobody's victim. I took her seductive bedtime-story voice, made it my own.

"You want to tell me why you did all this for me?" The voice floated out of my mouth, touching the Ds and Ts so lightly, like keys on a child's piano. A perfect impersonation of Dr. Sydney Stark-Leiffer. "This room and . . . everything else?"

Pierce looked at me, his expression softening even more. "Because . . . I . . ."

"Go on. . . ."

"You know why. I can tell from how you look at me."

"We have a spiritual connection, don't we?"

"You don't belong with John. He leaves you alone in bed at night." He moved closer, stared into my face. His breath was antiseptic—from mouthwash, or kissing spray. "John doesn't care who comes in when he's gone. He doesn't care who watches you . . . sleeping."

I cringed. *Stay with me, Sydney.* "The night Marla was killed, John was gone all night," I said. "Why were you in her apartment rather than mine?"

"If you go into her closet, the coat closet, next to the door? There's a spot in the back corner. It still smells like you." He leaned on one arm, gazing at the side of my face, and I thought, *Pillow talk. That's what he thinks this is.* "Marla Soble died because she decided to hang up her raincoat." He grinned. "Nikolas died because he was a better blabbermouth than a spy, and Gundersen . . . Well, you know why he died. Not an ounce of body fat on that guy. I see why you liked him."

I stared at his lower lip, still shiny red on the spot where I'd bit him. "Where did you get the blood . . . for Marla's valentine?"

"That's your valentine, not hers." He got up on his knees, and slowly, he took off his T-shirt. I remembered Fiona saying, *"All the cutters I've ever known have been girls."*

If she could see this, I thought as I looked at a collection of thin, even scabs about two inches long, running across the width of Pierce's pumped-up chest, between the nipples, as if he were keeping score of something. There were three rows of them. "These are for you, too."

"You cut your chest for me? I don't understand."

"Ever since you knifed that perp, I've wanted you," he said. "No, that's not right. I've . . . worshiped you."

"But how was I—"

"Each line is for a time I saw you, or had dinner with you, at John's apartment. It's blood from my heart."

"That's . . . romantic."

"Each time I made a cut, it was to stop myself from doing what you made me want to do."

"What did I make you want to do?"

"What I did to Marla. And what I did to Nikolas, and Nate. And my mother. And John."

I gasped. "John?"

"Sorry. I mean what I'm *going* to do to John."

He left the room for a moment. When I saw him again, he was holding the cordless phone in one hand and his knife in the other. And he was smiling.

The smile grew broader as he hit the redial button. "Hey, buddy, guess what? She showed up. Yes, isn't that great news? And she says she's really sorry about freaking out. . . . What's that? You want to talk to her?"

Pierce held the receiver to my ear while placing the knife at my throat. "Sam?" said the voice on the phone, as Pierce touched the tip of the blade to my skin. *Please, not Krull,* I thought.

"Talk," Pierce whispered.

"John," I said.

"I'm so glad you're all right," he said. "That camera. We have to find out who—"

"Yes," I said. "We do." *Please don't let him be next. Please don't let Pierce carve him up and take digital photos of him.*

"Tell him to come," said Pierce, as the pictures from the camera flashed through my mind like a sick slide show: the bloody heart on Marla's wall, Nate's carved-up abdomen, the woman's bleeding leg (Marla's leg? Pierce's mother's?) against that dull pink background. A dirty, stained pink background, it was . . . *It was Pierce's shag rug.*

I said, "I know you didn't take those photos. You could never do that to that woman's leg."

"I could never do any of that, Sam. But we have to find—"

"I couldn't look at that leg either."

Pierce said, "Tell him."

"Come get me, John. We can all figure this out together."

"Okay . . ."

Pierce took the phone away and hung it up. "Nice work," he said. "And you're right. He could never do any of that."

What if Krull didn't understand what I was trying to tell him? What if he doesn't know me well enough to take a second look at that leg photo, or doesn't recognize the setting? "I'll make a deal with you," I told Pierce. "Let him go, and I'll stay here with you forever."

"No, he has to die."

"Why?"

"Well, for one thing, you're gonna stay with me no matter what. I might as well have my cake and eat it too."

"But . . . I want to tell him to leave and never come back."

"I'm not buying that."

"I mean it, I—"

"I don't know why you care so much about him, anyway. He's a cheater, just like Soble."

"He's . . . what?"

"He's been seeing his ex-wife."

I tightened my jaw, summoning shock into my eyes. "He doesn't have an ex-wife."

"Yes, he does. Didn't you see all those letters in his safe?"

"I . . . I was too focused on the camera."

"He has an ex-wife and a son."

"I don't believe you."

"You know those times when you have no idea where he is?"

I nodded slowly.

"That's where he goes. I followed him once. Or maybe it was fuckin' Nikolas who did it; I don't remember. She lives in Brooklyn. Park Slope."

Through my teeth, I said, "Does he love her?" This felt so bizarre, acting out a bad soap-opera scene while bound and handcuffed to a green bed in a green room, a scarecrow on the screen of a green TV, singing about his missing brain.

I heard movement in the hallway. Pierce dashed out of the room to look through the peephole. "Took him long enough," he said when he returned.

I pulled against the cuffs, fear rushing through my body like blood before finally transforming into the false anger, the outrage, I needed. *Act like a murderer and he'll treat you like one.* "I want to help." My voice was so tight and vengeful it actually surprised me.

He turned and looked deep into my eyes. "You mean . . ."

"I want to help you kill him."

Slowly, Pierce's mouth twisted into a grin. I smiled back as he unfastened my feet, my hands, and I followed him into the front room.

As we stood in front of the door, I talked to him in the same voice Sydney had used when she thought I was Sarah. Intimate, loving. "You do know me, and guess what? I'm just like you. You can see inside me, so you know. You're the only one who does."

He produced a gleaming switchblade from his pocket and handed it to me. "You remember how to use it?"

Thank you. "Of course I do."

Krull knocked on the door. "Zach?" He knocked again.

"It's open!" Pierce hollered.

"Ex-wife, huh?" I said, and Pierce smiled and nodded as the door creaked open.

Krull walked in, a loaded gun held straight in front of him. "Put your hands up over your head now," he said.

But Pierce was too close, too fast.

He pulled me to his sweaty chest, held the polar-bear knife to my throat. "You tipped him off, you bitch."

"No, she didn't," Krull said. "I figured it out myself."

"How?"

"From the way you fucking act around her all the time."

"Bullshit."

"You really want to know? I took a saliva sample from one of the beer cans you're never throwing away and I got a match for the DNA on Marla's wall."

Pierce stared at him, unmoving. I turned my head a fraction of an inch, and whispered in his ear, so low only he could hear it, "I'm just like you." His grip loosened a little, but not enough. Not yet. The cold hilt stayed pressed to my sternum, the blade still sharp against the thin skin of my throat.

"Let her go," Krull said.

Pierce said, "Drop the fucking gun."

"Let her go first."

Pierce leaped at Krull, the switchblade straight in front of him, sticking it in Krull's chest as he fired off a shot. "Missed!" said Pierce, pulling out the blade. And as I watched Krull collapse to his knees, blood pouring, spreading throughout his yellow T-shirt, the muscles in my legs tensed up. My veins hardened and numbed with pure, true rage.

I plunged the blade into Pierce's bare back, into the soft spot between the scapulae.

"Oh . . . fuck," Pierce groaned, and fell to the ground.

"See?" I said. "I'm just like you."

Before coming over, Krull had called for backup and, within minutes, uniforms and paramedics were rushing past the bewildered neighbors, peering out of cracked-open doors.

Both detectives were carried out on stretchers. Krull was nearly unconscious from blood loss. But Pierce, ever alert, ever overreactive, stared at me with wide, unblinking eyes. "I'll be thinking about you," he said, and touched a hand to his lips, still stained with my blood.

I rode in the back of Krull's ambulance, holding his cool, dry hand as paramedics hovered around him, pressing a tourniquet to his gushing chest wound, fitting him with IVs. "Please live," I said, over and over and over.

Just as the ambulance arrived at St. Vincent's Hospital, he squeezed my hand. I looked into his pale face and, for a fraction of a second, his eyes opened and he said something.

I thought it was, "Okay." But I wasn't sure.

An hour later, a bespectacled young doctor in bloody blue scrubs walked out into the waiting room and stood over me, staring for half a minute. Then he said, "He's stabilized. He'll be fine."

I exhaled. "Oh, thank God. I thought you were going to tell me—"

"Yeah, sorry about that long pause," he said. "I'm kind of delirious with exhaustion, and I thought for a second you were Sydney Stark-Leiffer."

They moved Krull out of the ER, and into a regular hospital room, and when they finally let me in, he was propped up on pillows, looking pale and tired, but alert.

I felt a powerful sense of déjà vu—of Krull in the same hospital, a bullet wound in his neck, a year and a half earlier. "Would you do me a favor and stop bleeding for me?"

Krull said nothing—just smiled, slid to the side of his narrow bed and lifted the covers. I got in beside him and took his hand, the one that didn't have the IV in it.

And for a long time, I stared up at the ceiling, just feeling Krull's hand, listening to his breathing until I started to drift off.

Krull said, "I couldn't look at that leg either." His voice was so whispery thin that, for a moment, I thought he was talking in his sleep.

"What?"

"I couldn't look at that leg either. Look at that leg. I got it. I saw Pierce's rug in the photo."

I looked at his face. "You mean you didn't run a DNA test on him?"

He turned his head toward me, smiling. "I only run those on you."

I kissed him, very softly, and then we closed our eyes. We fell asleep in the hospital bed, breathing in and out in unison.

EPILOGUE

What Scares Me Now

In the months following Zachary Pierce's arrest, those who didn't like him—Patton especially—liked to say, "I told you so." But the real truth was, when it came to Pierce, nobody told you, or me, or anybody so.

Most people found him mildly annoying, a little weird at the worst. He had his eccentricities—the gleaming head, the gym addiction, the strange fact that he never took his T-shirt off, even in the shower—but none of these seemed like warning signs, even to his seasoned, cynical colleagues. Every last one of them thought his mother's death the previous year had been a suicide.

Before his arrest, there were only two people

who knew the real Zachary Pierce, and that was Katia Stavros and her son, Nikolas—a sweet, smart boy who played chess for money in Washington Square Park, before realizing he could make a lot more money selling crack.

Pierce had been drawn to the building first, because it was the perfect place to stake out my classroom. The building led to Katia, Katia to Nikolas. Pierce knew a lost soul when he saw one, and pounced. He started leaning on Nikolas almost as soon as he met him, asking him to watch me, follow me, report back on what I did on a daily basis.

For that, Nikolas got a small, weekly stipend and the promise he'd never go to jail again, no matter how much crack he sold in the park where he used to play chess. As an added bonus, Pierce bought him a pair of binoculars.

But Nikolas saw the rages, which occurred when Pierce thought I'd looked at him the wrong way, or had shown too much affection toward Krull. Nikolas knew what had happened to Marla, and that scared him into action.

His mother had asked him to stop sending me those notes, to stay out of the policeman's business. But he didn't listen, and Pierce found out. Just like he found out about Jenna's suspecting Nate and I had slept together. Just like he found out about Krull's ex-wife and son. That was the irony—Pierce was a better detective than anyone ever gave him credit for.

He's awaiting trial, with a hotshot female lawyer who's already dropping hints about an insanity plea. For the time being, Pierce is living on Riker's Island, separated from the rest of the prison population for his own safety; former cops are never popular in jail, especially when they've killed women. He hasn't read the interviews with Katia in the *Daily News* and the *New York Times* because he's denied access to all print and electronic media. But according to the *Post*, he's been getting bags of fan mail.

A week after Pierce was arrested, Krull and I went to Nate's funeral together, and sat alongside Jenna and Ezra. "Does Uncle Nate get to take all those flowers to heaven?" Ezra asked as the minister spoke and many of his beautiful costars— male and female—wept into handkerchiefs.

"Sure, honey," said Jenna. "He gets to take his Emmys, too."

Nate's three older brothers were there, all of them handsome in that Nordic/Minnesota kind of way, but none so sparkling as their brother had been. As they lowered the casket into the ground, I watched Nate's parents, staring at that closed box so raptly, as if they were still hoping, somehow, for a happy ending.

Sydney didn't make it to the funeral. She flew out the next day. Yes, *flew* out, because she was living in California. She'd never left.

WLUV was broadcasting her via satellite, and the whole "live" thing was just a publicity stunt that entailed some sort of confidentiality agreement. "You should have told me," I complained during her visit, over glasses of wine at the Stanhope's bar. "I wouldn't have said anything. And besides, I'm your daughter."

"Oh, Samantha," she said. "You of all people should know I'd never move to New York. You know what the humidity does to my hair."

She'd never even thought about moving, as it turns out. Yet so many other changes have occurred in these two short months: Yale got the part in *The Mikado*, with the director's caveat that he "Please lighten the hell up." Shell broke down, said, "Screw the ring," and started sleeping with En again. And, in a truly surprising turn of events, the actress who played Juliana left *Shakespearean Idol* to portray Blythe's long-lost sister on *Live and Let Live*—and was replaced by none other than Tabitha—sorry, Tabs Meeks.

I've changed too, but on the inside and not really for the better. Here's what scares me now: Sterling roses, *The Wizard of Oz*, polar bears, the color green, collages. Clowns too, but that's an ongoing thing.

Also, if a stranger pays me a compliment, or if any straight guy, other than Krull, looks into my eyes for more than three seconds, I start to hyperventilate.

I know I'll feel different someday. But when you're bound to a bed with a bald killer straddling your chest, it's going to make an impact. Right now, there's love, and then there's that other, awful emotion—the one you have to watch out for.

I haven't met Ethan yet. Sheila thought we should take it slow—but that's going to change today. Krull has him for the whole weekend, and I'm meeting the two of them at the playground on Twelfth and Seventh, where Sheila likes to drop him off. I have to say, I'm nervous. Before Krull left our apartment this morning, I asked his opinion on four different outfits, all of which he very unhelpfully called, "Fine."

I'm heading west on Twelfth now, in my fifth outfit—a red hooded sweatshirt under a peacoat with jeans—which I'm feeling pretty good about, though my heart is pounding harder than it ever has on any date, even my high school prom. I really hope he likes me.

I reach the playground and spot them immediately: Krull standing at a distance as Ethan inches up one of the tallest playground slides I've ever seen.

"Dad?"

"You can do it," says Krull.

Ethan nods, then takes the ladder one step at a time until finally he reaches the top. From my experience as a preschool teacher, most kids want an audience when they scale a height like that. "Watch this!" they yell. "Look at me! Look how high I am!"

But when Ethan gets to the top, he just slides right down—no announcement, not even a pause. Just that look of pure joy, then completion, as his shoes hit the sand.

"One more time!" he says. His eyes are so much like his dad's that it breaks my heart. Then Krull turns and waves and I think, *Family.*

As I start walking toward them, I feel a chill up my back—that unsettling sensation of being watched by someone, somewhere. But for now, I see Ethan smiling at me, and I'd rather ignore it.

Turn the page for an excerpt from
Alison Gaylin's
debut suspense novel

Hide Your Eyes

The first novel to feature
Samantha Leiffer and John Krull

PROLOGUE

Your Spiritual Lifeboat

"I'd kill for publicity like yours," said Shell Clarion yesterday morning. Shell has said this many times within the past month, but I've never responded because it annoys me in so many ways.

First of all, there's the tone: I'd *kill* for publicity like yours, as if she were talking about metabolism or pore size.

The truth is, when you're in the papers, everybody stares at you. You can't buy things like condoms or facial depilatory cream. And you can forget all about spitting, or saying "fuck you" to a bike messenger who nearly knocks you unconscious, or doing anything even remotely unphotogenic, because you *will* be noticed and it *will* make Page Six of the *New York Post* under some self-fulfilling headline like "Is the Pressure Getting to Her?" and then you'll be even more paranoid than you were to begin with.

There's also the unspoken implication that I should be doing something with this publicity—writing a book, for instance. I don't want to write a book. I want to teach prekindergarten and work in the box office of an off-Broadway theater. I've been doing both for years, and neither requires a spokesperson.

Most important, there's the fact that I *did* kill for publicity like mine, and if Shell honestly wants a bunch of cameras shoved in her face when she's buying tampons at Rite Aid, all she needs to do is kill someone too. But she has to understand this first: No amount of publicity can make up for the dreams you have, every night, after you take someone's life.

Of course, I didn't tell this to Shell, because she is an aspiring soap opera actress who *chose* the name of Shell Clarion, and you don't want to discuss existential pain with somebody like that. So instead I said, "I bet if I punched you in the face, we could both make the six o'clock news." Worked pretty good. Wish I'd said it earlier.

My name is Samantha Leiffer. Even before the killing, the last name sounded familiar to people because of my mother, Sydney Stark-Leiffer, self-help author and lover of publicity.

In her latest book, *Your Spiritual Lifeboat,* Sydney talks about the simple ways we can all stay afloat in "the sometimes placid, sometimes roiling sea called living." Meditation or prayer is the life vest—"the puncture-proof floatation device that you wear close to your heart." The planks of the lifeboat, described in the following fourteen chapters, include self-education, exercise, career fulfillment, family, laughter and friendship. The rudder—the thing that gives the boat direction—is love.

Sydney's sold about a trillion of these books, so I hate to disagree with her, but my lifeboat has always been constructed differently than that. Until recently, it consisted of two planks getting tossed around in a choppy ocean, with me lashed to the top. The planks were my two jobs. Love was the school of hungry sharks circling just below the surface. Forget about the life vest; the sharks would swallow it whole.

The odd part is, love was what brought me to New York in the first place. I'd met Nate during my senior year of college when I stage managed *King Lear* and he played Edmund the Bastard. He was so freakishly beautiful, Nate. A shimmering blond museum piece, with brains and talent and an ass you could rest a full martini on, and he claimed to love me. I guess I'm attractive, but not like Nate. Nate literally caused traffic accidents.

I'd often wake up in the middle of the night and stare at his closed eyes—almond shaped, with thick, honey-colored lashes—and wonder, *What is wrong with him?*

Turned out there *was* something wrong with Nate—or, at least, with Nate and me. I found out after I'd followed him to New York and taken the job at the box office and learned, through a series of cryptic answering machine messages and a bouquet of irises on the doormat, that he was screwing his commercial agent, Susan, every day after I left for work, and his theatrical agent, Gregory, on Monday, Wednesday and Friday evenings, when he was supposed to be at his Method class.

Through my mother's most recent ex-husband, a real estate developer, I found a decent-sized, lower Chelsea studio on the twelfth floor of a pre-war building, overlooking an airshaft but rent stabilized. Then I called a furniture rental place called Rent 2 Own and ordered a roomful of blond wood and beige cushions. The idea behind that decision was: light, modern, very temporary. Yet I wound up renting the stuff so long I owned it, and found myself stuck with an apartment that looked like a dentist's waiting room.

Still, the place was convenient. Only ten street blocks north of the Space, which is the theater where I work; an additional three avenue blocks east of the Hudson River, where I like to take walks; five street blocks south and two avenue blocks west of Sunny Side Preschool, where I began teaching a year after the breakup, when I decided my lifeboat needed a sturdier, more buoyant plank.

Unconsciously, I'd arranged my life in a tight, safe circle in which even subways were unnecessary. I had my kids to keep me company from eight 'til noon; my aspiring actor coworkers at the box office to entertain me from two 'til curtain. Then I had a microwavable dinner on my blond wood dinette in front of the Shopping Channel, and bed.

My mother said I wasn't realizing my true potential. "Who moves to New York City to teach nursery school?" she'd ask over the phone from L.A. "Who goes to Stanford to work in a box office?"

I don't know, Mom, I'd want to reply. *Who gets divorced three times in six years and then writes a chapter called "Love Is the Rudder"?*

Mainly, I was happy—the kind of muted happy that you don't notice at the time, but see clearly after it's gone.

*   *   *

There are seven people, including the manager and me, who work in the box office of the Space. That's about six too many. But in a textbook case of putting the cart before the horse, the rich owner believes a busy box office attracts big ticket sales. Or so she says. I think it's a tax scam.

Before I tell this story, I should list the names of my box office coworkers. The kids at Sunny Side have normal, human names like Daniel Klein and Nancy Yu. When I introduce them, you won't go, "What?" and stop paying attention to the story in order to digest the syllables. The Space staff, though—aspiring actors—have the most blatantly changed names this side of the porn industry: Besides Shell Clarion, there's En Henry, Argent Devereaux, Yale St. Germaine and Hermyn. Hermyn is a woman—a feminist performance artist and the only person I've ever met with just one name. Each of us has a cubbyhole near the will-call window, for phone messages, mail and notes from visitors. On top of each cubbyhole, there's a piece of masking tape with our initials on it. Hermyn's just says "H."

Until last month, Hermyn never spoke. Not a word. She'd taken a three-year vow of silence in order to shore up vocal power for *Inanimate Womyn,* a one-person show in which she mutated her voice into a whip, a brick and a feather.

My other coworkers thrill to the sound of their

own voices. That includes my best friend, Yale St. Germaine, but I like the sound of his voice too.

When the rest of them have been sniping and singing and pontificating so much that it seems they've stolen all the air out of the room, Yale invites me outside for cigarette breaks. Even though he knows I don't smoke. Even though everyone knows I don't smoke. "How about some secondhand carcinogens?" he says. And I run.

Life would've been so different had I chosen to not smoke with Yale on that overcast day in February when I took a walk to the Hudson River instead.

I still wonder what made me stop at that ugly, abandoned construction site in the first place, let alone stay long enough to see what I did. Initially, I assumed it was boredom, or PMS, or possibly the loneliness that used to hit me so often, especially on overcast days in late winter when *everything* looks ugly and abandoned. In interviews, I've attributed it to claustrophobia—an occupational hazard for anybody who works in a box office. But lately, none of that seems right.

I've been thinking it was luck. Whether it was good luck or bad, I'm not sure.

1

Squad Watery

It was Valentine's Day, or, as Yale St. Germaine liked to call it, "the only holiday with a massacre named after it." Valentine's Day depressed Yale because he'd had some gorgeous ones in his life—the kind with roses and candlelight and someone with moist eyes grasping both your hands over a white tablecloth and comparing you to various addictive substances.

I'd never taken Valentine's Day seriously. It was fine for my preschool class, but to my eye it was a kids' holiday, full of sweet but unsubstantial things like paper hearts and candy. And boyfriends.

The only valentine I could depend on was the one from my mother. It was the same postcard her publicist sent out to the media: a black-and-white headshot of her taken circa 1981, the year her first book came out. In the white space over the photo hovered a pink, cursive inscription: *Open Your* ♥ *and Love Will Sail In.* Despite the two decades that had elapsed since the shot was taken, Sydney looked more or less the same. Like me, with an Adrien Arpel makeover.

Because she still used it as her author photo, it had attained icon status among Stark-Leiffer enthusiasts: the sculpted, dark hair with its warm, professional-looking highlights; the pale eyes, embraced by kohl; the outlined and painted lips compassionately pursed. It was a photo that said, "I know how to accentuate my best features, but right now, I'm thinking about *you.*"

Sydney usually just scrawled her signature on my valentine, but this time she'd added a note. *Have fun, Samantha,* she'd written at the bottom of the card in bright red ink. *Please.*

I was carrying the card in my giant patchwork shoulder bag as I walked to Sunny Side that morning. And I was also carrying more February Fourteenth fun than Sydney Stark-Leiffer could shake her red pen at: twenty cut-out valentine hearts, five extra pads of construction paper, one bag of children's scissors, eight packages of doilies, two jars apiece of red, silver, gold, green and pink glitter (and three extra jars of gold, because the kids loved gold), nine tubes of Elmer's glue and twenty small boxes of crayons.

It wasn't tons of fun, but it felt close to it. Who knew paper products could be so heavy? It couldn't be helped, though. My classroom had been robbed twice. (I still found this hard to wrap my head around. A gang of West Village nursery school marauders.) In the latest heist, they'd made off with all my Chanukah decorations—including the Styrofoam latkes and the giant paper dreidel—so I was relatively certain valentine supplies wouldn't be safe there overnight.

I shifted the heavy bag to the other shoulder, and that's when I felt it. A creeping, cold sensation originating at the base of my spine, winding up through my vertebrae one by one, settling into the sweat on the back of my neck and pressing against it, like puddled ice. For a few seconds, I couldn't breathe.

A man bumped into me as he passed. "Get the fuckin' fuck out of my fuckin' way!" he said. It always amazed me how many times New Yorkers could insert the word *fuckin'* into a sentence, and normally I would've stared at this man, if only to see what someone who said "fuckin' fuck" looked like. But I was too distracted. The awful tingling began to dissipate, though the idea of it lingered.

Dead Man's Fingers. Chills up your spine for no reason. The sign of a bad premonition.

I don't like to think of myself as superstitious, but I am. It comes from my grandmother, who lived with Sydney and me after Dad moved out and chastised us if we wore socks around the house. *(If you wear socks with no shoes, you'll lose all your money!)* Grandma was forever spitting, muttering oaths, knocking wood and tossing salt over her shoulder. My mother thought it was obsessive-compulsive, but I bought right into it.

Ten years after Grandma's death, I still didn't wear socks around my apartment. Occasionally, I whispered *keinahora* to ward off the evil eye.

When you feel Dead Man's Fingers, you're supposed to stop whatever it is you're doing and do the opposite. That way, the premonition might not come true.

For me, doing the opposite would have meant turning around and going home. I imagined myself calling the principal, telling him, "Sorry, Terry. Dead Man's Fingers."

I tried to attribute the sensation to the bitter February cold, to a forgotten bad dream, to Valentine's Day with no valentine. But then it returned, this time in italics: *Dead Man's Fingers.*

I removed my bag again, shifted it to the other shoulder. *Maybe that'll suffice as doing the opposite. Suffice for whom? What am I thinking?*

I pulled my coat closer to my body. It was the

same coat that I always wore on cold days—a heavy, black, men's wool coat that I bought at the army/navy store when I first moved to New York—and I found comfort in its enormity. It was about four sizes too big, because there is no such thing as a man (especially an army/navy man) who is my size: five-foot-one, one hundred pounds. For some military reason I'm sure, this coat had a hood, which I never wore because it made me look like a Druid. But one block away from Sunny Side Preschool, with Dead Man's Fingers stuck in my nervous system and the sickening certainty that something horrible was going to happen, I pulled the hood over my head until it obscured the top half of my face.

I need protection, I thought. It seemed to make sense.